# ESCAPE

## THE LAZARUS ALLIANCE: BOOK ONE

## BLAZE WARD

KNOTTED ROAD PRESS

Escape
**The Lazarus Alliance: Book One**
Blaze Ward

Copyright © 2020 Blaze Ward
All rights reserved
Published by Knotted Road Press
www.KnottedRoadPress.com

ISBN: 978-1-64470-130-0

Cover art:

ID 25138013 © Philcold | Dreamstime.com

Cover and interior design copyright © 2020 Knotted Road Press

**Reviews**
It's true. Reviews help. Even a short one, such as, "Loved it!" So please consider reviewing this book (and all of the ones you've read) on your favorite retailer site.

**Never miss a release!**
If you'd like to be notified of new releases, sign up for my newsletter.

http://www.blazeward.com/newsletter/

**Buy More!**
Did you know that you can buy directly from my website?

https://www.blazeward.com/shop/

## ALSO BY BLAZE WARD

**The Lazarus Alliance**

*Escape*

*Return*

*Rebellion*

**The Jessica Keller Chronicles**

*Auberon*

*Queen of the Pirates*

*Last of the Immortals*

*Goddess of War*

*Flight of the Blackbird*

*The Red Admiral*

*St. Legier*

*Winterhome*

*Petron*

**CS-405**

*Queen Anne's Revenge*

*Packmule*

*Persephone*

**Additional Alexandria Station Stories**

*Siren*

*Two Bottles of Wine with a War God*

*The Story Road*

**The Science Officer Series Season One**

*The Science Officer*

*The Mind Field*

*The Gilded Cage*

*The Pleasure Dome*

*The Doomsday Vault*

*The Last Flagship*

*The Hammerfield Gambit*

*The Hammerfield Payoff*

*The Bryce Connection*

**The Science Officer Series Season Two**

*Alien Seas*

**The Handsome Rob Gigs**

*Can't Shoot Straight Gang*

*Can't Shoot Straight Gang Returns*

*Hunting Handsome Rob*

*Handsome Rob, Assassin*

**Shadow of the Dominion**

*Longshot Hypothesis*

*Hard Bargain*

*Outermost*

*Dominion-427*

*Phoenix*

*Princess Rualoh*

**Hunter Bureau**

*Mirrors*

*Latency*

# CHAPTER ONE

## CAPTAIN

IT WAS AN OLD HUMAN ADAGE, dating back well before men ever took to the skies, let alone the stars: *A captain goes down with his ship*. Especially an experimental warship design like *Ajax*, pushing the envelope of science every direction, almost into the realm of magic.

Alone, this one Starcruiser should have been able to take on an entire Patrol of Westphalian Phalanx vessels: four Phalanxes and an Archer, with an expectation that he could crush them. Unfortunately, they'd blundered into a full GunWall while during this shakedown cruise: sixteen Phalanxes, four Archers, and a CommandWall.

And still given better than they got, but it hadn't been enough.

He would have coughed as he looked around the smoke-filled bridge and considered his impending death, but the vacuum suit he wore kept everything clean and crisp, in spite of the death and mayhem that had occurred around him. The last of his surviving crew were finally blasting their way clear in the escape pods. He had remained behind to contemplate his failure. Standing orders called for him to arm the scuttling charges right now and blow himself and his final command to kingdom come. However, he knew doubt.

Perhaps even fear.

That a Westphalian scientist would somehow be able to piece together enough of the wreckage to understand what he and his team had managed here. That they might manage to build their own version of Kirov's Lance, a weapon as much superior to the standard Star Lance as that beam was to the much smaller Star Spear. Worse, Westphalia would use such a weapon, perhaps such a ship to conquer the rest of the sector, when the Rio Alliance was just trying to halt the Westphalian invasions.

He took a look around. The damage hadn't befallen them fast enough that any of the corpses of his crew remained here on the bridge with him, but he knew that their ghosts would haunt him angrily for denying them a proper burial at sea in a place where their kin could perhaps come visit one day.

But his duty came first.

"This is your final warning, *Ajax*," the Westphalian CommandWall vessel, the ship in charge over there, transmitted triumphantly.

He hadn't surrendered, even when it was inevitable. Just ordered his crew to abandon ship and prayed that the Alliance would be able to trade them home eventually.

Without him, most of the rest couldn't tell Westphalia anything they hadn't been able to read off their own scanners already. An experimental warship, compact and deadly enough that Westphalian officers would warn each other about what had happened today.

They could be taught fear as well. Doubt. He just had to make sure the lesson would stick.

He unbuckled from his command seat and staggered across the bridge to where a starpilot had died not five minutes ago, when a shot finally speared the bridge hard enough to kill *Ajax* as well.

There was still blood on the chair and station as he sat, the remains of his pilot that would stick to the outside of his suit, but that was the cost of surviving this day. Of exacting some level of revenge on the very gods of fortune that had dropped the two forces into each other's laps.

He programmed the star drives to a spot where the scans had shown brightness. A star-birthing nebula so dense with gases and new fusion lights that they would never find his corpse or his ship, to discover what had happened today. *Here There Be Dragons* kind of place.

All the power that had been running the Kirov got channeled into the star drives instead, leaving the shields as strong as they had been for most of the battle.

He stared once more at the shattered, staggering remains of a Westphalian GunWall, and smiled.

He didn't believe it for a moment, but he still snarled the thought at them, as if his terrible rage alone would be enough to touch his enemies from beyond whatever grave he was about to consign himself and his ship to.

*I will return for you.*

And then he slammed a palm down on the controller and leapt into infinity.

# CHAPTER TWO

## CAPTAIN

*AJAX* HAD NOT FAILED HIM, even as he had failed her. Somehow, the coordinates he had programmed into the star drives, a random mishmash he had expected to carry him to his death inside a newborn star, had brought him out instead in the middle of a dark, hollow space.

It was like finding a park amidst the overpacked slums of Greenbriar, back home on Brasilia, the capital world of the Rio Alliance. A little pocket of green and beauty nobody had ever imagined might exist.

He cracked open the faceplate of his suit to study this wondrous place without the extra glass in the way. Around him, the bridge blowers and fans were sucking up the smoke and death scent that had filled the air of his bridge and replacing it with something that almost smelled like a forest, compared to the battle with Westphalia. That would be the vertical farm hydroponics facility midship, but in imagination, his memory, he wandered those slums of his childhood.

Everywhere around him, the robots and repair systems would be furiously working. He knew it was wrong to ascribe emotion to them anthropomorphically, but he couldn't help thinking that perhaps *Ajax* was as enraged as he was that the gods of fortune had killed both of them on their very first cruise, before they had a chance to show the Rio Alliance and Westphalia what a warship like *Ajax* was capable of.

He was supposed to be dead now, they both were, yet even that had been denied them.

Again, he wondered if a spy had leaked the coordinates of the test mission. That it had been an ambush from the start and not just random, entropic luck. No other explanation made sense as to why an entire GunWall might drop out of jump on top of him and his ship.

He owed somebody a debt of pain and retribution, but the mailing address was blank, for now. He could live with that. Those same gods had apparently chosen him to live long enough to deliver it personally.

Internal systems showed the breakdown. Almost all of his brand new vessel was damaged to some extent. Nothing but the star drives and a few sensors were fully functional, even now.

Still, the ship could repair itself reasonably well, given time. Another secret that must be hidden from the Westphalian scientists, how to impregnate fluids and certain microbes into a carbon-nanotube/steel matrix that would repair itself, given time and raw materials supplied by service robots his engineers had jokingly dubbed *gardeners*. Spray water and fertilizer, and keep watch to make sure the systems stayed within their programmed bounds.

He needed to kill it all. Destroy this ship now that he had escaped Westphalia, so that they couldn't reverse engineer his secrets and eliminate the surprise innovation that might let the Rio Alliance win enough of the war to push the Earthers back into their own sphere. At least until they decided that they didn't need to conquer the galaxy.

A captain went down with his ship. The ultimate price to pay for failure.

His hand hovered over the switch that would arm the scuttling charges and send them both to hell.

He still knew doubt.

Had the meeting truly been an accident. Or a spy? He knew that the Alliance would consider him dead with his ship. Lost at sea, as it were. The corpses that remained behind with him would join him on that roster.

*On patrol.*

The ancient saying that indicated a naval vessel that had sailed into the wide oceans of distant Earth never to return.

He could not make his hand complete the circuit. Could not destroy *Ajax*, even as she lay fighting for her life around him. In four months, perhaps eight, depending, she might be as good as new if he left the robots and circuits alone. And that spy, whoever he was, might have been rewarded by Westphalia for destroying *Project Ajax.*

On the pilot's board in front of him, a light appeared.

Coherent radio signals, out here in the middle of a box of stars so close and bright that he still didn't know how he had managed to not hit anything in his blind flight. Perhaps he was truly a poor man, and had indeed entered the Kingdom of God, for he had apparently passed a camel through the eye of a needle to land in this place.

None of the signals were pointed at *Ajax* as near as he could tell. The light-speed burst of his arrival, that flash of azure light against the night sky, would be hours reaching the inner portions of the system he had blundered into.

But radio suggested intelligence. Civilization. People, at least of some sort, as his target had been farther from the home colonies than any human vessel had ever transited, to the best of his knowledge. Only his own desperation had driven him to such an extreme decision.

He listened. Voices. Languages he didn't recognize, but the very act of hearing something on a radio frequency was bizarre enough. Another first contact?

Humans were not alone in the universe. Their own radio waves had enticed other explorers, until the two sides found each other. But this wasn't the Interlac of the Rio Alliance he was hearing. Nor the Anglo-Germanic of the Westphalians.

This was something else. Something that might be friendly, and might not be. He had no way to tell.

Around him, *Ajax* went to work with her mindless dedication to service. To the war itself, which would free the Rio Alliance from the Earthers of Westphalia, those men and women who felt that alien species should be subjugated, rather than welcomed.

And if he was already dead, did he have anything to lose?

He did not. All options entailed risk, but perhaps, just perhaps, the Kingdom of God had offered him a second chance.

If he was mad enough to risk it.

# CHAPTER THREE

## LAZARUS

HE HAD DECIDED to take on a new name, reflecting the raw miracle of his escape. Of his failure to die when all the odds favored it.

Someone obviously had a greater plan for him, to have shown him the way forward at the very moment when he was prepared to do his duty as his superiors back home had impressed upon him. He would survive, at least as well as he could. As long as he could.

In his rebirth, he went back to his youth and chose the name Lazarus, for another man who had been dead and then returned to life by a miracle. It was arrogance itself on his part, so he crossed himself and prayed for forgiveness.

If he could buy himself six months, survive that long alone in an alien star system, *Ajax* would be as repaired as she could be without a stint in the bio-dock to fix everything else.

But she would need secrecy. That much was obvious.

The reaction thrusters were running at around thirty percent efficiency. That was enough for now. He spun the bowsprit around and killed his velocity, relative to the closest star of the nine within a few light-years of him. Lazarus headed inward at a slow pace, listening to the signals and recording them.

Hopefully, somewhere in their chatter, there would be a key that would allow him to start translating their tones into communication. Moving at this speed would give him time, if he was careful not to be seen from below. Optical telescopes were watching the night sky constantly, and had already noted a few moving stars in the firmament of the heavens below him.

Planets. Big ones, too. Ice giants, this far out, but that would be the perfect spot to hide *Ajax* while he figured out what to do with the aliens who did not know he was eavesdropping on them.

Lazarus slept for a time. Listened to the alien chatter, which sounded like nothing so much as a pair of pilots bored and talking back and forth occasionally as their ships maneuvered closer together. Truck drivers making a delivery somewhere they had been to before.

He visited the cold storage area and converted it to a morgue for his friends and crew. *Ajax* had gone to space with only ninety-seven sailors aboard, small for a warship of this power. Casualties had still been atrocious, as he looked down at the twenty-eight dead before him. Hopefully their ghosts would only haunt his dreams and not his days.

A full day passed as he slept, ate, and worked, listening all the while.

Finally, the ship entered into orbit of an ice giant so distant that the local sun was barely brighter than two of the closer neighbors. Lazarus shut down as many systems as he could, running silent into night as the ship circled the blue-green marble below in a complicated dance with a whole tribe of little moons.

Down on the flight deck, he loaded up the one dispatch boat with supplies. Naval architects back home called it a *koch*, after the ancient Russian boats capable of sailing the pack ice. This one had a short-range jumpdrive, meant to handle personnel runs and mail, rather than the two bigger boxes, known as *pinckes*, aboard to serve him as cargo shuttles.

Alone, the space felt enormous, as the koch was designed for a pilot, an admiral, and an aide. Six might fit for short missions, if they were friendly. One almost bounced hollowly around.

Lazarus added a laser pistol and a bolter rifle to his gear and dug out his armored lifesuit, heavier than the simple suit he had been living in, leaving the faceplate retracted. It would handle any EVA tasks if he needed to, but better to run on the koch's life support for now.

Just in case.

He felt a twinge of pain and separation as he backed the little ship out of the launch pod and aimed his bow straight up, relative to the plane of the system. Once he got enough distance to be comfortable with the local gravity wells, he jumped a quarter light-year, which put him nearly a fifth of the way towards one of the stars that direction.

A second jump dropped him back into the first system, but at a random enough location with no backwards vector that would point someone to *Ajax*, hopefully.

Alone in the darkness he listened. If they were watching the skies around them, the blueshift of his arrival would show up on sensors and in portholes fairly quickly. The koch was unarmed, if they were pirates, but nothing he had heard so far suggested that.

Miners, maybe, operating in the asteroid belt he had detected, similar to the one around many systems, where a proto-planet failed to live up to its potential.

Just because he had no other choice, not really, Lazarus opened the transmitter on the channel the two voices had been using most frequently and spoke.

"Escape-Pod-Two-Seven-Three-One to local vessels," he said simply in Interlac, prepared to trigger the jumpdrive to blast him into deep space again if they turned out to be hostile. "Please reply on this frequency."

Just under nine seconds later, all chatter ceased as the two voices recognized that a stranger had joined them, and their last words echoed into silence.

Lazarus had spoken in Interlac. The aliens who welcomed the first human colonists to their worlds had claimed that Interlac was a near-universal tongue for all creatures capable of communicating that way. At the same time, that blob described an area of space only about seven hundred light-years wide and less than two hundred thick. And well away from here.

*Ajax* had carried him far beyond even the most ambitious limits of space the Rio Alliance and their friends had explored.

The koch had enough sensors to track what appeared to be two vessels over there, at least as they separated. He sent a scanner ping downrange and noted the return signal.

They would know where he was now, in addition to him arriving uninvited to their party. But Lazarus was a dead man trying to survive. He didn't have enough food to endure the time it would take for *Ajax* to repair herself and sail him home, unless he found help.

"Who is this?" a rough voice came back over the line, speaking Interlac with an accent Lazarus had never heard before. "What are you doing here?"

"I escaped when my ship was torn apart in a jump accident," Lazarus replied, trying not to sound evasive as he lied to the very people who might rescue him. "I'm lost and trying to make it to somewhere where I can find my way home."

That part was true. He just needed half a year for *Ajax* to be ready to carry him. What could she do to a Westphalian patrol force with a little surprise next time?

One of the two ships over there blinked out of existence as he watched. The other turned this direction and Lazarus felt his breath catch as he looked at the image on the scanner.

Every starship he had ever seen, even local spaceships, had always been built in a symmetrical manner, usually mirrored on the sides, if you sliced it down the long line of the center.

This stranger was not. It almost looked like a treble clef from a page of music. Or maybe one of those ancient sea monster ammonites, curled away to the starboard side as it turned a head towards him. The engines were in the middle of the left side as the ship spiraled back, with a goose neck and head coming from the starboard part of a circle.

He had never seen anything like it.

Around him, the koch suddenly shuddered and crunched as light flashed from the enemy vessel. The strangers had fired on him.

It was a trap.

On his boards, the jumpdrive was dead. The engines were failing. Life support cut out with an eerie silence as he listened.

"What are you doing?" Lazarus yelled at them as their ship fired a second time.

Metal tore, and he could see space and stars through a gap where hull had been.

Red lights signaled an impending failure of the generators.

Lazarus reached between his legs and triggered the ejection system. It was meant for failures at low altitude in an atmosphere, dating back to aircraft flying skies without ever reaching space. But nobody had ever changed the basic logic.

A rocket ignited and the roof of the cabin detonated outward on a set of charges that opened the rest of the cockpit to space.

Lazarus was pressed tight as the rocket carried him to safety, where presumably a parachute or something equally irrelevant in deep space would try to stop him from slamming into a nonexistent planet nowhere below him.

In space, there is no sound, other than your own harsh breath as your faceplate detects a pressure change and slams shut to save your life. The rockets stopped after a few moments and Lazarus was coasting.

He twisted around enough to watch his second command die for real this time, a silent flash of light and radiation that left very little in the way of salvageable rubble.

Or evidence, if you wanted to look at it that way.

The other ship, the strange alien curve that looked like nothing he had ever imagined, drew closer.

His seat was slowly turning, so he unbuckled and kicked off against it to kill some of the spin and watch the other ship following him.

The suit's onboard systems detected some sort of scanner beam. It must just be a scanner, since it hadn't chopped him into pieces.

"What species are you?" that strange, almost-angry voice pursued him across the cosmos. "You aren't Innruld."

"Human," Lazarus replied. "I have never heard of the Innruld."

"You speak their tongue, stranger," the voice growled.

"Where I come from, it is called Interlac," he countered. "I was told it was the common tongue of deep space."

Silence.

"I am an unbelievably long ways from home," Lazarus said, trying to convey however many hundreds of light-years that might be with just his tone.

"And we have never heard of your kind here, human," the voice replied gravely.

Lazarus decided it was a male voice, for reasons he could not explain. A captain on that ship, possibly up to no good and angry at being discovered.

If they were evil creatures, they would have already killed him, like they had his ship.

Unless their goal was to let him float in space until his suit gave out and he died while they watched.

There was always that.

Lazarus felt something take hold of his entire body, bringing him to exact rest relative to the ammonite. For a moment, he fancied that he could see faces in the section that stuck out from the front, where lights glowed out of a wide viewscreen.

Underneath that, he could see what his brain kept calling a ball turret with guns pointed right at him. Waiting like a bird dog sniffing in the morning mist.

"Are you a cop, human?" the voice asked.

Cop? A gendarme? Here? Were these folks criminals after all?

"No," Lazarus replied firmly. "If anything, I probably qualify as a rebel."

"Against whom, human?"

"Westphalia," Lazarus replied. "I doubt you've heard of them either, but they plan to take over all of known space, given the chance. I was fleeing them when my other ship died."

"Well then, human rebel, let us see if you are worth rescuing," the voice laughed roughly.

Lazarus felt an invisible tug, drawing him forward. Below, the strange ship rotated on her y-axis, a yaw that brought an opening around to line up with him and light up internally.

Airlock? Or mouth?

Shortly, he would find out.

# CHAPTER FOUR

## ADDISON

ADDISON SIGHED INTERNALLY and tried not to growl his angry thoughts as he uncoiled his lower half and slithered off the command coil where he had been supervising the cargo transfer.

Wybert had panicked. He did that. All that aggressive adrenaline overloaded the Ilount goofball at times and he attacked where other species might flee. That was what the Ilount did. It was probably why the Queen sent all her males out into space, keeping only the females behind to maintain the nest.

An Ilount Queen wanted mighty heroes to mate with. The survivors usually qualified.

Addison didn't know if Wybert's tremendous luck made him eligible, as the fool was a barely-contained berserker at the best of times, a goofball at the worst, and with a tendency to shoot first and forget to ask questions later.

Still, he usually made a good gunner for *Shiva Zephyr Glaive*, but Addison realized that he needed to maintain a shorter leash today to keep Wybert from killing people before they needed it. Should have locked the guns from the bridge.

Addison flexed his narrow shoulders backwards until they touched, to relieve some of the stress as he undulated his lower half once around the command coil, working out kinks in his tail.

"Kuei, keep us still relative to the alien while the energy web pulls him into the airlock," Addison ordered his Helmsman, a female Vaadwig with a better sense of three dimensional maneuvering than anyone he had ever met. "You're in charge up here for now."

She turned and smiled at him. He thought it was a smile. Her narrow, long skull was covered with tan fur instead of proper green and blue scales, and had external ears larger than his hands, sticking out and up from the sides of her head. Those ears moved like flags in a breeze, but he had known her long enough to read the woman's mood and nonverbal communication.

"We're stable, Director," she nodded.

"Cormac, plot an escape course back out of the nebula by a different path than we normally enter," Addison turned to the small box forward to port, the dock where his ancient NavCrawler plugged itself in to plan pathways through the stars.

"*We have six programmed presently, Director,*" the little bot replied, always referring to itself in the plural for reasons Addison had never gotten it to explain. "*Do you exhibit a preference?*"

"Furthest away from normal by physical space," Addison replied after a moment. "The colloquial long-ways-around."

"*As you command, Director.*"

Addison started to depart, and changed his mind briefly. He slithered back to the command coil and opened the intercom to cover the entire ship.

"Wybert, disarm your guns and meet me at the airlock

with your spear," he ordered. "Everyone else without duty get weapons out of the locker and do the same."

He closed the channel and slithered over to the bridge arms locker. Churquen like him didn't have hips like some of the upright species, especially the Innruld, but his kind had long-since mastered a leather harness that put everything within reach. He draped the bandoleers in place over his sleeveless tunic and locked them, and then added a compact pistol where a biped might have a hipbone.

The creature they were bringing aboard was a biped, but of a type that didn't show up in any records. Much shorter than an Innruld, although of the same basic mechanics. But almost as heavy as the overlords of the galaxy, from the readout.

Addison wouldn't bother with melee combat if the creature was unruly. He would shoot it, or let Wybert and his stupid powerspear loose on the human. Addison could always coil his lower half around the creature and squeeze it to death if it got to that.

Out the bridge hatch, he heard his crew moving around. There weren't any more Churquen besides him, and thank the fates themselves that he only had one Ilount crew member. Addison could only imagine two of them on one deck, each constantly trying to one-up the other.

He'd probably end up having to space the pair of them at some point, just so he could sleep.

Khyaa'sha emerged from her kitchen on the deck above and descended over the rail on a line of web as he approached. She was a Tarni, what others occasionally called a cartwheel spider, and could always bite someone with those smiling mandibles. Plus, while she walked on all eight legs, at least until she arrived somewhere, she could still rear up on the back six to free her front pedipads for delicate work, like folding strudel pastries.

Today, she had a beam rifle slung along her abdomen along with her own pack harness. Organic webbing coiled from a hook on her harness if she needed to tie the human up. She could always make more on the fly.

Addison would have liked to have Ereshkiki Nisab, his Qooph Systems Mechanic, at hand, but the wheelman would be busy keeping those poor engines from overheating and breaking down.

The last thing Addison needed right now was to be stranded in the middle of a nebula with a cargo of illegal narcotics destined for an Innruld world.

Aileen and Remahle met him at the airlock, the former still dripping water from her fur as she pulled a vest around herself and then drew a pistol. Aileen was a biped, of sorts, like the stranger. Fur-covered, like Kuei, but the Yithadreph were marine mammals for the most part, with short legs and arms emerging from a long torso. She must have been asleep in her bunk, floating peacefully, when he woke her.

And if she was dripping on his deck now, it was his fault for ordering her to move, so Addison might just mop it up himself later as an apology.

Remahle was also a furred mammal, but a much lighter brown color than the nearly umber of Aileen's. Also a biped, but nearly a head shorter, coming up only to Addison's shoulders. Also about as nimble as Aileen. Innruld generally referred to the Kr'mari derisively as glider squirrels. Where Aileen wore pants with several big pockets on the thighs to go with pockets in her jacket, Remahle had a harness similar to Addison's, except it went around his neck, down his chest, and around both legs, so as to not interfere with his glider membranes.

The clacking of Wybert's ten feet on the deck signaled the approach of the lunatic gunner. Addison checked that the man was holding his damned powerspear with both of his upper arms, which would hopefully keep him from drawing the pistol on his hip and randomly shooting the human. At least before Addison ordered him to.

Both antenna were at attention today, almost like horns, and all four mandibles were clenched shut, like combat was imminent. Five eyes glared out at the world in challenge. At least the lower arms were resting on his belt, below the chest armor Wybert wore over his chitin to anchor the saddlebags he had slung across his lower thorax.

"I want the human alive, unless he attacks us physically, Wybert," Addison growled at the Ilount warrior. "You've already cost us the value of whatever that ship was."

"I said I was sorry," Wybert squeaked back defensively.

The species might be more impressive if their voices weren't like birds chirping. Even an Ilount who stood five and a half feet tall and another seven feet from keelbone to pooptube, plus the foot of gripper spinnerets beyond that.

Addison could rear back and look down on Wybert when he needed to impress the creature. Hopefully, it would not be necessary.

"Where's Thadrakho?" Addison asked, looking around for his last crew member.

"I have him back here helping with a fluid leak," the calm, stone tones of Ereshkiki Nisab came over the intercom.

"Acceptable," Addison replied.

A working ship was more important than an additional creature to impress the human, even if a Necherle like Thadrakho might be the most scary, according to some of the stories Addison had heard. Necherle were a cold-adapted, insectile species taller than anyone else on the crew, covered over with a chitinous hide that insulated them. Thadrakho was a pretty good junior systems mechanic. Better than anyone else, anyway.

The outer airlock hatch had sealed and the room finished

pressurizing as Addison looked at the giant in the chamber beyond on the screen display. Now they would find out what manner of fish they had caught.

# CHAPTER FIVE

## LAZARUS

LAZARUS KNEW the day was going to be even stranger as soon as the whatever-it-was deposited him inside the steel-and-light maw on the side of the ship.

Airlock. More or less. Weirder than any version he had ever seen, even in the kind of low-budget vids that the fleet shipped out to all ships for entertainment on a regular basis. Even to secret bases developing cutting edge warships.

This was the first one he'd ever seen that was round instead of squared off. And it opened in an iris, rather than a big, heavy plate that would seal up in an emergency.

The lights in here were also dimmer than he would have set them, but that was a personal thing, rather than a mechanical issue.

But it was the gravity that warned him. Maybe eighty, eighty-five percent what he was used to on a daily basis. He would have to be careful not to accidentally fly if he jumped too hard, at least until he got used to it.

His feet found the deck and he heard the exterior hiss as the airlock did its thing and inflated reality around him. Lazarus watched his sensors register the change. Oxygen content a little higher than he was used to. A couple of weird trace gases he wasn't, but nothing that would poison him.

So far.

His laser pistol was attached to the exterior of his armored lifesuit, with the flap down and the magnets that had held it through an ejection-into-space cycle. He left the bolter rifle slung across his back as well. The locals might be hostile, but they might not, and looking like he was threatening them with an act of piracy was no way to get their help.

At least not yet.

Finally, a series of lights and sirens burped at him, probably warning anyone in the area that the airlock was about to open. He turned towards the inner hatch and flipped up his faceplate, but left his suit running. Bottled air, just in case.

The inner hatch irised open.

Lazarus was struck by a nightmare vision he couldn't have steeled himself for, even in his worst dreams.

They were monsters.

Bizarre, alien creatures.

The closest one had four arms, ten legs, antenna, and blue skin. But he was also carrying a long spear in his top two hands, and had it pointed into the airlock.

Next to him was a naga from ancient, Hindu mythology on Earth. Scale-covered in green with long, blue stripes, the lower half of the body was a snake tail longer than Lazarus was tall. Vertical, it had two, spindly arms from narrow shoulders, a head with large eyes and mouth, and maybe those slits were nostrils. It had no ears, but it was wearing a crossed bandoleer with pockets and a pistol of its own.

A giant spider with black hair and red stripes stared malevolently at him from beyond those two, its head and front arms up with what he assumed was a rifle of some sort in its hands.

Next to it, a dire sea otter in pearl-colored Capri pants and a banana-colored vest held a pistol on him. She also dripped water onto the deck. At least there were shoes on her feet, unlike the rest.

And she was most definitely a she, even for a fur covered otter. She had breasts like a human woman. Or at least bumps in the right location and shape.

That just made it weirder.

Next to her, almost at the back, was a ring-tailed lemur with bat wings.

*What the hell are those trace gases? Did they flood me with hallucinogenic drugs?*

"What is your name, human?" the naga asked in a deep, rich voice that Lazarus remembered from the radio.

The captain of the ship, maybe. Or the Communications Tech.

And it spoke in Interlac, albeit with a strange accent unlike any Lazarus had ever heard in the Rio Alliance.

But he was also a thousand light-years from home.

"Lazarus," he answered, standing perfectly still so the legged slug with the spear didn't suddenly rush him.

Lazarus was pretty sure his armored lifesuit could stop a simple spear, if the creature hit him in the chest plate, but it might go after the softer joints and open something.

God Above only knew what kinds of alien diseases he might pick up in an open wound.

It didn't do his sense of well-being any good when everyone over there jumped just a little as he spoke. Them being nervous might be worse than them piratical, truth be told.

He wanted to cross himself again, for thinking unethical thoughts, but now was not the time. They might think he was a sorcerer, or something, in spite of everyone standing on a starship talking.

"How did you come to be standing on my deck, Human Lazarus?" the naga asked.

It had been a day. Several days. A whole week.

Getting *Ajax* ready for her trial run to test everything. The sudden fight to the death against an entire GunWall. Suicidal flight and survival. Aliens.

His head came up a little and his jaw jutted. Just a little.

"Somebody blew up my escape pod," he said sourly. "My ship was already destroyed. I'm so far from home I'm not even sure that I can get back there in my lifetime. And then you came along."

The centipede thing started to move. Lazarus could see it in the way the antennae on his head tilted forward suddenly. The way the ten feet all seemed to flatten themselves against the deck, as if gripping for a charge. The hands shifted on the spear.

Lazarus put all his focus into his right hand. He would step back, open the flap, draw the laser pistol, and go for the thing's head. Blind it at least, and then use the airlock door to keep the others from rushing him.

"Wybert," the naga snapped angrily, turning his head to look at the creature and ignore the human for a moment.

"Sorry," the thing said in a voice so high Lazarus almost laughed.

It settled its weight back and grounded the spear on a metal cap that looked like it contained some sort of machinery, from the lights Lazarus saw on the side of it. Good to know it wasn't just a stick with an arrowhead on the end.

"You claim to be a rebel against something called Westphalia, Human Lazarus," the naga captain turned those two, vertically-slitted eyes his way again.

Lazarus kept waiting for a forked tongue to flicker out.

"That's right," Lazarus finally said, when he realized no tongue was coming after him. "They are a group of human supremacists that believe all aliens should be subjugated or destroyed. My nation, the Rio Alliance, has been fighting them for years. The non-humans we know taught us Interlac, this language. They said it was the language all spacers knew."

"What species have you met in this Rio Alliance, Lazarus?" the naga asked.

At least the others were calming, if he read the body language correctly. The blue centipede was actually leaning some of his upright weight on the spear as a pole, rather than preparing to kebab one lonely human with it.

"Moah," he answered. "Gnashiiley. Atomarsk. Those three are the most common, but there are supposedly dozens of others. I have never, however, seen any of your species, I think."

"Atomarsk are a legend!" the spider with the black ruff and the beam rifle yelled angrily at him.

Something about the face suggested female, and that made sense, since black widow spiders were always female in his nightmares.

Carefully, Lazarus held out his left hand at shoulder height.

"About yea tall?" he asked. "Maroon fur and a tail fan made up of seven feathers?"

The woman spider gasped. The beam rifle fluttered just a little, making him wonder if she was about to shoot him.

Hopefully, aliens around here understood safeties on guns. And used them.

"Have you heard of the Innruld?" the naga, the captain if Lazarus had to guess, asked sternly.

"I have not," he replied. "Not until you asked me about them earlier. You say I look like them?"

"No," the naga shifted some on his…tail.

His coiled tail that reminded Lazarus of a rattlesnake on a flat rock, preparing to bite. Even a green one that looked more like a garter snake that ate bugs and slugs in your garden if you were nice to them.

"You are much shorter than the self-proclaimed Lords of the Galaxy," the rattlesnake captain said. "As heavy, perhaps, though. And your hand has four fingers instead of three. But the similarities are close enough, as you are otherwise a biped of a standard model."

Lazarus wondered what a *standard model* implied, but it didn't seem politic to ask at the current juncture.

"And a lost sailor in need of rescue," he said carefully, hoping that the ethics of spaceflight were the same everywhere. Or close enough. "I may not know your technology, but I am willing to learn, and work for my passage someplace."

The whole group bristled. Gun hands gripped a little tighter. Gun barrels wobbled around in response to the twitch in the arm holding it.

"Do your kind take slaves, Human Lazarus?" the commander over there asked.

"I'm fighting a war against those kinds of people, buddy," he growled back sharply. "Is that what you think bipeds do?"

"It's what the Innruld do, Lazarus," the naga said sternly. But then he smiled. "However, if you are willing to work, we might find a place for a rebel."

Lazarus didn't really like the chuckle that emanated from the group, but he didn't have much choice at this point.

# CHAPTER SIX

ADDISON

ADDISON WATCHED the human carefully as he spoke. The spacesuit covered much of his body language, making it difficult to read the alien's reactions, but the face seemed extremely emotive through the open face plate.

Wybert was relaxed, so it was likely that the human would survive this encounter, unlike his ship, which had exploded into millions of tiny, glowing fragments when Wybert got too excited.

Pity. What would an alien starship have been worth in this sector of space?

"So I am Lazarus," the human stated, locking predator eyes on him. "By what name should I address you?"

"I am Addison Wolcott," he replied, letting the muscles of his mouth and eyes stretch into something approximating a biped's smile. "Director of this vessel: *Shiva Zephyr Glaive.*"

To see how good the human's memory was, he decided to introduce the rest of the crew currently present.

"Wybert of Capantzina," with his powerspear for whatever close combat might occur on a starship. But you didn't separate an Ilount from his spear without getting him drunk first.

"Remahle Mebarsu is a Kr'mari," as the flier half-bowed with an opera cloak for effect.

"Aileen Enjehn is a Yithadreph," Addison smiled. "Your first job might be mopping the deck dry for her, since I ordered her out of her bed for this."

The human nodded carefully, apparently studying Aileen closer than the others. That made sense, since she was the closest to him in terms of evolutionary trees. Erect, fur-bearing bipeds, and all that.

"Khyaa'sha Ramarkhay is usually our cook," Addison smiled at the woman and wondered what a human might eat that they would need to lay in, next time he picked up supplies.

If Wybert hadn't blown up the human's ship, they might have been able to remove all of his food. Addison wondered if anything *had* survived the explosion that they might salvage now.

"Ereshkiki Nisab and Thadrakho are in the engine room at the moment," Addison added, letting the human know that there was more crew about. "And Kuei Akeley is on the bridge flying."

Addison tensed his whole body now, studying the way the human stood. Not completely at ease, but also not preparing to fight Wybert to the death either.

"You appear to be armed, Lazarus," Addison said carefully. "Wybert will put your weapons into the armory for now, and your suit will go into storage with the rest of ours. Do you have personal clothing you can wear?"

Most bipeds wore their space suits instead of clothing, plugging various orifices into tubes in such a way that basic clothing got in the way.

This would be where they determined if the human would serve, or die. Would he give up his weapons and submit himself to non-bipeds, or would Wybert have to distract the big human with the spear until the rest could engage?

The human paused, eyes averted. A heavy breath escaped its mouth.

Slowly, oh so slowly, it lifted a long weapon on a strap from over his chest and leaned it against the side wall. The pistol's holster was attached to a belt that buckled in the center.

*Weird. Doesn't it get in the way when folding yourself in the middle?*

Still, Lazarus wrapped the belt around the weapon and held it out with one hand towards Wybert.

"I have clothing, but it is stashed in a backpack and I can't get to it until I unsuit," the human mused.

Addison had second thoughts and looked around.

"Aileen? Would you?" he asked.

She glanced at him then nodded in a compact jerk that said much about her nerves in approaching a monster, nearly a quarter taller than her and possibly twice her weight. But the alternative was Wybert right now.

Addison didn't feel like having to mop blood out of the airlock if the fool Ilount reacted badly to something accidental. And he might. Ilount were not deep thinkers.

Addison didn't have his pistol aimed directly at the human. Not yet. His reflexes could center it faster than Wybert could blink, if he needed to. Aileen would probably collapse to the deck if she panicked, so he should have a clear shot.

Center of that torso would probably fail. It looked armored and Addison had no idea what humans might consider tough. But the faceplate was open. If nothing else, he could permanently blind the monster on the way to spacing him.

Aileen sidled into the airlock and slid to her right. She only had a stub of a tail, but it was up against steel right now.

Lazarus held the weapon out as far as his arms would reach without moving his feet and let her snag it and quickly retreat out of the airlock.

"I am unarmed," Lazarus said, carefully enunciating his words so they were clear, in spite of the guttural accent he had. "I am about to open my suit. It will make strange noises and panels will open apparently at random. This is necessary. Is it safe to exit the airlock and do this where you are standing?"

That last, focused not on Wybert, like most people would be, but on Addison, the Director holding Wybert's metaphorical leash tight right now.

"It is," Addison decided. "Come."

He slithered backwards, away from the hatch and deeper into the Main Deck Primary Cargo Hold. Aileen and Remahle joined him quickly. Khyaa'sha went up the outside of the ramp to the balcony overlooking the hold. If the human moved to here, she could drop on him in a heartbeat.

"Wybert," Addison barked at the Ilount, gesturing for him to back up.

Ilount could walk backwards. It took a lot of coordination and attention, things Wybert did not excel at, so he looked like a drunk Kreeghal when he did so.

At least he moved.

Lazarus exited the airlock and entered *Shiva Zephyr Glaive* proper. He looked around him with an eye that told Addison the human was used to starships, and perhaps knew quite a bit, from the spaces his gaze lingered.

Still, Lazarus did not move suddenly or dangerously, perhaps understanding that the Rules of Hospitality only stretched so far.

"Stand by," the human said simply.

# CHAPTER SEVEN

## LAZARUS

TRULY, an alien starship, somewhere more than one thousand light-years from Earth. Crewed by aliens of a variety of types Lazarus had never even dreamed about, let alone encountered. Naga. Decapeed. Glider. Swimmer. Spider.

What other insanity awaited?

Still, he was the guest here. Lazarus made eye contact with Director Wolcott and nodded politely, hoping the body language was universal. The naga nodded back.

Lazarus reached up and keyed the sequence of external switches that would unlock his helmet. A twist and it popped loose, hanging just from the lanyard at the back. He detached it from the bolt and set the helmet off to one side. An emergency suit was designed for quick entrance but short duration, so he had chosen the armored lifesuit.

Might have saved his life, considering the explosion that killed the koch.

Next, the six latches along each side of his ribcage that always reminded him of the lorica breastplate of the ancient Roman Legions. He keyed the upper arm release and his arm coverings split just above the elbow, with the top half retracting into the shoulder joint. Front and back plates detached at the waist as well, and he lifted it over his head. It went next to the helmet.

Lazarus looked around and found a bench. He could do this next part standing in a pinch, or sitting on the floor, but he'd slept in the suit, and his muscles were stiff.

He wondered if the aliens had a tub big enough that he could just soak in hot water. The dire otter, Aileen, probably had something, but that might be her personal bed. And she was still as tiny as an eight-year-old human girl.

He sat and began keying secondary functions. His forearm coverings retracted into bracers attached to his gauntlets. Thigh rings slid down, over his knees, and into his boots. He sighed as he pulled each boot off and wiggled his toes. Gauntlets next, and all he had on was the abdomen base with the plumbing controls.

Lazarus took a deep breath and triggered the release, grunting and flinching as everything detached and retracted. At least it was less uncomfortable than attaching everything.

He stood and slid the last piece to the floor, standing stark naked in front of a bunch of aliens.

The backpack on his armor had a pouch for clothes, folded tight and vac-sealed up in a tiny bag. He pulled it out and tore the seal.

Shirt, jacket, pants, socks, underwear. The shoes would inflate over the course of an hour and then the soles would harden overnight and he could wear them in any environments that the jacket was sufficient for.

If it got that cold, you were supposed to stay in the suit with the heater on anyway, for as long as the batteries and fuel would hold out.

The aliens hadn't moved. It was like watching a bunch of

statues in a garden, except these blinked occasionally as he got dressed.

Whoever had packed this emergency kit for him had been into reds. Crimson-colored pants. Jacket matching the pants, with gold piping and a logo for a beer company embroidered in gold thread on the left breast. Off-white shirt not much different than Aileen's pants, with the same logo printed this time on it.

Seriously? A brewery?

But then he supposed that such a company might have paid to have their logo go everywhere as part of an emergency kit. Cheap advertising.

Lazarus made a note to go find them, one of these days, and see if their beer was any good. Plus, anyone recognizing the logo would have had to come from closer to home, so they might be able to help.

He reminded himself that he only really needed six or eight months for *Ajax* to be good enough to make it home. He could fly her by himself, but combat would require a full crew.

Did he dare recruit any of these aliens to come help the Rio Alliance?

He was dead, after all.

Lazarus chuckled to himself as he stuffed his new shoes into the thigh pouches on his pants and began to gather up his lifesuit.

"What tickles your fancy, Lazarus?" Aileen asked timidly.

He stood and faced her, pointing to the logo on his chest.

"I'm wearing emergency clothing designed for people going into an escape pod," he smiled, tapping his chest. "This is a brewery on Brasilia, my homeworld. They make beer, and probably paid someone to put this here. I am now a walking billboard."

"Beer?" she asked, her brows growing together in apparent confusion.

"Several kinds of grains fermenting in water to an alcohol level around six or nine percent," he replied, remembering soberly how far from home he was.

Interlac didn't have such a word, so he had automatically used the Spanglish term that had originally traveled to Brasilia with the colonists, itself an offshoot relative of the Anglo-German of Westphalia. *Cerveza.*

"You drink poison?" her brown eyes got huge. They were quite expressive, when he studied her face. And her whiskers had all leaned forward, as if tasting for danger.

"In low doses, it is an intoxicant to my kind," he said. "At least methyl alcohols. Ethyl alcohol is indeed poisonous."

From the reactions over there, folks around here must not drink hooch of any kind. He wondered what they did to relax. Everybody ingested something. Or smoked it. Or chewed it.

*Right?*

"What do I do with all this?" he gestured, holding the various pieces of his suit in his arms.

The decapeed, Wybert, stepped around him and Aileen, making a beeline for the bolter rifle. It should be safe, as Lazarus hadn't put a bolt in the chamber. Hopefully the creature was smart enough not to just randomly do things to the weapon.

Depending on where he pointed it, Lazarus could see a shot penetrating the outside hull from here.

"Come with me," Wybert said, holding his spear, the pistol, and the rifle in his four hands and rippling in the direction Lazarus interpreted as forward.

Nearby was apparently an armory. Guns have a specific look to them, and physics is physics. Lazarus figured he could use at least half of these in a pinch.

"What do I need to do with the pistol to make it safe?" Wybert asked as he opened the doorway.

Lazarus considered offering to show him, but that might make people nervous right now.

"Remove it from the holster and hold the handle with your fingers around the large part that sticks out at the bottom," Lazarus said, watching carefully and prepared to leap to the side if the barrel came around this way.

Wybert drew the pistol. His hands were close enough to human that it was a pretty good fit.

"That is the trigger," Lazarus pointed. "The safety is the red switch above your thumb. Down would be armed. Up is safe."

It was safe, for the moment.

"On the other side, there is a button if you pull your trigger finger back, above the trigger," Lazarus continued, waiting for the Ilount to turn the weapon over and see it. "Press that and the powercell will unlock and slide out of the hand grip."

Wybert followed Lazarus' instructions. His whole body rippled with surprise as the cartridge moved out a bit and then hung on the rails.

"Pull gently, and it will come the rest of the way out."

And just like that, Wybert had mastered a laser pistol. He nodded sharply and smiled up at Lazarus. It looked like a smile. The four mandibles, like fingers with sharp claws at the end, opened up like a flower briefly and then clacked shut again. Considering how stern he had looked earlier, Lazarus took this as a good sign.

"To disarm the bolter rifle, just depress the red switch on the front of the piece that sticks out perpendicular at the base," Lazarus smiled back at the man. "This is a bullpup configuration rifle. It fires ammunition contained within the magazine in the rear stock, and I did not charge it with a round previously."

Pop, and the Ilount was holding the laser pistol, the powercell, the bolter, and the magazine in his four hands, with the spear leaned against the wall.

"Here," Aileen leaned in and tapped him on the shoulder. "Wybert will be some time playing, now that the weapons are safe. Let us put your armor away, and we can clean the floor."

Lazarus followed her back to the chamber next to the airlock and found a shelf to put his parts. His unconscious had been expecting spacesuits, but for humans. Nothing else here would fit a human, but he could identify the crew member, just from the shape.

The two he hadn't seen must be utterly frightening. One suit was made for a pencil nearly seven feet tall and skinny enough he could wear his own suit and then put Lazarus's armored lifesuit on around that.

The other suit was a drum, split open sideways and waiting for someone to climb in. Two spindly arms emerged from the hubs and reminded him of cat tails with six finger claws at the ends, all facing inward.

*Momma, I'm a long ways from home.*

The others had disappeared for now. He had heard them moving away in a strange symphony of footsteps on the floor.

Aileen found a towel for herself and dried her fur after she handed him an old fashioned mop with a squeegee bucket.

Lazarus shrugged and set to work, earning his supper.

# CHAPTER EIGHT

### ADDISON

ADDISON HAD HEADED across the main cargo deck to the engine room. Thadrakho was nowhere to be seen, but that just meant the leak was inside a wall somewhere, or in the overhead plumbing again.

Ereshkiki Nisab rolled back from the console and blinked several of his eyes.

Qooph. The Wheelmen.

One of the oldest races to have achieved starflight, even before the Innruld came and forged their empire on the backs of the non-bipeds.

Addison wondered how one of the overlords would react to a human in their midst. Probably badly. Lazarus had none of the characteristics of beauty that the Innruld demanded of themselves.

Ereshkiki Nisab rolled to a stop and deflated one of his ring pockets enough to rest. Addison had never understood the evolutionary pressures that forged the Qooph. His Systems Mechanic had once said that they evolved up from simple ground slugs, in the way that the Churquen had once been snakes.

But the Qooph had added a bone and cartilage endoskeleton. Formed into a pair of hexagons attached at the hub, with six bladders around the outside that they could inflate and deflate to roll forward or backwards as needed.

Four feet tall. More than two feet wide at the hubs. Solid and stable, everything a Churquen might want in a Systems Mechanic.

Two thin arms stuck out of the axle, ending in hands with six opposed thumbs and no wrist. They could not lift much, but were among the most delicate artisans in the galaxy.

Between the twin outer rims, six eyes and six mouths were equally spaced around the inner rim. Ereshkiki Nisab studied him now with two eyes and a grinning mouth.

"The human passed inspection?" he asked with at least four mouths from the harmonics.

"He does, for now." Addison finally allowed himself a sigh. "You would have needed to see him without the armor to understand how dangerous his kind must be."

"Oh?"

"He might outweigh you, old friend," Addison said. "Certainly any two of the rest of us, excepting only Wybert. He is at least six feet tall, and weighs nearly two hundred pounds, most of it being muscle. And he walked like the gravity in here was almost too weak for him."

"Warrior?" Ereshkiki Nisab asked, blinking and focusing. Both hands came together in front of himself like an old lawyer clenching his hands across his belly. It was not a Qooph mannerism, but one he had picked up in his years with non-rollers.

"Possibly," Addison nodded. "At least well-armed for a scientist or explorer. I have not yet probed his past. Aileen is putting him to work and the others are quietly watching to see how he reacts."

"Will we keep him?"

"I am currently obligated, Ereshkiki Nisab," Addison felt his eyes slit in a low-grade anger. "Wybert killed his ship and Kuei has not been able to identify salvageable bits. Even the Innruld would take him aboard, if only to put him to work, much as I have done. At least here he has a chance of freedom later."

"And the place he rebels against?" the mechanic asked. "Westphalia?"

"Kuei could find no records, but we've never looked," Addison shrugged. "I will quietly ask questions, but not until the current cargo is delivered. No use tempting the authorities."

"But you do not feel it is a trap?" the wheelman asked.

"Everything is a trap," Addison sighed again. "This one feels like less of one than the others. For now, we need to flee from this place in case our other friends panicked after delivering the package. I had told them that we would deal with the situation when Lazarus appeared. I can honestly say that we destroyed the intruder before he could escape to warn anyone of what he saw here. Hopefully, they will take that at face value."

"And if they do not?"

"We are all rebels, old friend, same as Lazarus claims to be," Addison finally laughed. "Who would they tell? The Innruld?"

# CHAPTER NINE

LAZARUS

HE HADN'T BEEN a midshipman swabbing decks in nearly two decades, but Lazarus had not forgotten how it was done. And he only had to get them dry now, rather than soaping, cleaning, waxing, and sealing them over the course of an entire day.

The Yithadreph woman, Aileen Enjehn, watched from a safe distance as he worked his way slowly through the space outside the airlock, past the storage and armory and other closed hatches, and into a hallway that ran at an odd angle to the rest. But then, nothing in this ship appeared square, except a few internal bulkheads.

This must be where the crew quarters were. He looked up from his work and saw a trail of water emerge from one of the cabins, presumably hers and she had been asleep when the alarm went up that they had a new passenger.

She had remained nearly silent as he worked, just leaned backwards against a handy wall with her arms crossed across her chest in something not quite disapproval but not all that friendly either.

The water was heavier here, so he worked with slower care to get it all up. Finally, he was working against the door to her personal quarters.

Lazarus put the mop into the squeegee and turned to face her as he wrung it dry through the ancient design of two wheels and a lever.

"I presume that there is more water through this hatch?" he said carefully.

"I will deal with it later," Aileen replied in a tone that managed to split the gap between defensive and angry.

But then, what woman wants a stranger to see her personal quarters, especially if they are messy? And he was a completely alien species on top of that, although they might both be mammals, at least from his estimation of her.

Still, Lazarus nodded and tried to smile at the tiny woman.

"What's the next task, then?" he asked, assuming they had more chores for him.

"Kitchen," she said, flexing her entire body to propel herself off the wall and back down the long corridor towards the cargo bay.

Lazarus left the mop here for now and followed her up a ramp where the black widow spider had gone earlier.

The space up here was an open balcony, curved around the upper deck of the cargo bay behind a rail with tables for a variety of species to all sit together and eat.

"Khyaa'sha," Aileen called. "He's yours next."

Aileen eyed him warily and slid around him to retreat down the ramp as the Tarni emerged.

Lazarus had no idea why a cartwheel spider might earn that name. She was the size of a really big dog as she emerged on eight silent feet and stared at him.

"Let us sit and talk like civilized beings," she said in a

voice that sounded like a woman he had once known on Brasilia, when he was seventeen and stupid. As opposed to thirty-five and marooned.

Lazarus found a bench-enough place at one of the tables and sat. Khyaa'sha walked close and leaned her weight back enough to rest on the rear of her abdomen and bring her front two feet in the air.

He had a hard time not reacting defensively when she did, as her head went up and those mandibles looked huge as if they were poised to strike at him.

*Deep breath. Alien cook on an even more alien starship.*

*I'm the weird one here, as far as they are concerned.*

"What do humans eat?" she asked simply,

As he caught his breath, Lazarus realized that their eyes were actually on a level this way. She was normally three feet tall and maybe six feet across all her feet. He was six feet tall, but a lot of that was torso, like most men.

Peers, seated. Huh.

"Humans are nominally omnivores," Lazarus said after a moment. "A variety of grains and vegetables. Meat and seafood that has been cooked at least somewhat to kill off certain germs. Fish can be eaten raw, depending on preparation."

"Do you really drink the poisons of a fermented grain?" she asked.

Looking closely, she had six small eyes around her skull, probably for defense, and two big ones centered above the mandibles. Hunter's eyes, like a human.

"The right grains, yes," he admitted. "Wheat, corn, rice, barley, hops, oats. I had a few emergency ration bars in my backpack, but nothing that will last me more than a few days."

"If allowed, I would taste one." She leaned forward just

enough to make him flinch, but that seemed to be attention, rather than threat. "It would let me find something similar to see if you can metabolize."

Lazarus nodded after his heart started beating again. He reached into a pocket where he had stashed them earlier and withdrew one. That left three. Maybe he needed to diet right now, anyway.

He held it out carefully with two fingers. Her pedipalp came up delicately and pulled it from his hand.

Exoskeleton, he presumed, although that big it might be dermal armor over an endoskeletal structure. She might weight eighty pounds, which would be light for a dog that size, to say nothing of a deer, but far too heavy for exoskeletal joints.

Khyaa'sha's chitin was covered over with fine, bristly, black hairs. The foot itself was a pad like a cat's, with webbed toes that moved like fingers and ended in claws smaller than his fingernails.

Delicately, this nightmare from his worst dreams tore open the ration bar and broke off a piece about the size of his first joint on his thumb. Up close, the two big mandibles covered four smaller ones, like Wybert's on the corners of an X. They moved more dexterously than fingers to grasp the sample from her hand and chew it.

"Sweet," she observed.

"We use honey from bees, an insect species back home," he tried to explain. "They digest pollen and water and produce a sweet fluid to feed larvae and such. Humans have slightly domesticated them to the point that they produce far in excess of what they need, and we can harvest it. It has a variety of antibiotic qualities, as well as being a significant energy source. And sweet."

"Very good," she nodded as those powerful jaws ground it up quickly. "Tree and ground nuts. Grains. A number of secondary chemicals added whose purpose I cannot identify."

"Mostly vitamins and trace minerals added to sustain a human who had access to only bars and water," he replied. "One bar and enough water will keep me alive for several days."

"Very well," she nodded again. "I will prepare a dinner of…"

Lazarus didn't know the word she used, but it had connotations of *dim sum*—Chinese finger foods—in Interlac. Lazarus repeated the word back to her with a question.

"Yes. Samples of a variety of things you can taste," she agreed. "Do you have sufficient medical supplies if I accidentally poison you for dinner?"

Oh, yes. Very much yes. That was the biggest part of the backpack, by volume. Things he should take now. Things he should have at the table with him. Things to take before going to sleep.

"I do," he said simply, planning a trip down to the storage room to get the rest of the backpack, once he knew where he might sleep.

"Good," she fell forward onto all eight feet and backed away from the table as gracefully as a cat. "We need to introduce you to Lenox next. He's our medic, and will need to work up records on you. Did anything survive from your ship?"

"I do not believe so," Lazarus replied. "Hopefully the Director will be able to find something of my previous life."

"My heartfelt apologies, Lazarus," she suddenly spun around to watch him with her hunter's eyes. "We are all refugees that way, so perhaps you will find a place here with us."

Lazarus nodded but remained silent. These folks might be refugees, but they were also shoot-first-ask-questions-later.

And the other ship had run like hell as soon as he announced himself, so Lazarus wondered if his new friends were criminals.

But then, what was he, in the eyes of Westphalia? And possibly the Innruld?

# CHAPTER TEN



IT GOT WEIRDER, which surprised Lazarus.

Lenox turned out to be a robot. Khyaa'sha called it a MedCrawler, and it was programmed with a cheerful Hippocratic Oath and the ability to shift its pronunciation down into an Interlac Lazarus could follow better than any of the others.

Khyaa'sha walked up a wall and hung herself in a corner of the space clear across the cargo hold from the airlock he had first boarded. Not far from engineering, if Lazarus understood the various cryptic references.

It would be interesting to see how the aliens moved. Maybe he could do things to upgrade *Ajax* from what he might learn here. Weirder, if he stayed long enough and ended up liking these people, maybe he could upgrade their ship before he left.

He was leaving. Lazarus hadn't worked out the when or the how, but he had the why nailed to a board. Westphalia.

The Earthers were probably aware that they had fought a new kind of vessel. That much they could get out of his old crew, especially the regenerative capabilities of this new warship. Those vessels would be looking over their shoulders for *Ajax* to return.

Patrols might even start looking for him, but all they had to go on was the original vector he had taken when he jumped, not the distance. And nobody else would be crazy enough, desperate enough to fly into a nebula like that without a charted path.

But that was tomorrow's task. Today, he had to worry about himself.

The MedCrawler before him was a red box, about a foot tall and two feet on the square. It really did have treads on both sides, when Lazarus would have expected wheels to be more efficient. But then, that was only on decks. Lenox might need to travel off the ship with Director Wolcott and his crew onto unknown terrain.

Each side and the top had folding arms and appendages: arms, tools, scanners, maybe even eyes, although it had enough of those around the rim of the square casing.

"So, Human Lazarus," Lenox extended a telescoping arm with several unknown devices on the end. "How would you classify your current medical condition?"

The voice was male. It reminded him of a nurse he had tried to recruit for *Ajax*, but the man had too good of a gig at the base hospital and wasn't bored enough for adventure.

Probably for the best, all endings considered.

"Stressed," Lazarus replied, looking down, even from the bench he sat on. "In addition to all the adrenaline of the last several days, I have now been exposed to alien bacteria and viruses that may or may not be able to cross species. My health was good at home, but I have also brought my own biome with me here and exposed your crew."

"Already noted," Lenox managed to smile with his voice alone as the one arm traced obscure Egyptian hieroglyphics in the air between them. "For baseline, describe your age and health levels."

"Human male," he replied. "We are a two-gender, mammalian species of erect biped. Age: thirty-five standard years, so just about at the peak of human development and potential, before age begins to slow me down both mentally and physically over the next six to eight decades. Oxygen breather. Blood based on iron hemoglobin. The gravity on this ship is about fifteen to twenty percent lower than what I am accustomed to, so I will need to find your workout equipment and see if it has a high enough top limit for me to remain in prime shape."

"Schooling?" Lenox asked.

"Rio Alliance Merchant Marine," Lazarus laughed. "That is a very thin disguise for a military university that I'm sure does not fool Westphalia. Advanced training in military sciences and experimental, mechanical biomorphics."

"I am not sure that latter term translates into Interlac cleanly," Lenox said. "Could you repeat it?"

"I probably should not, Lenox," Lazarus smiled down at the robot. "I doubt you actually have a high enough security clearance to know those things, and I would be surprised if my knowledge in the field would be applicable aboard this vessel. Or any others. *Ajax* was a bleeding edge experiment."

"*Ajax?*"

"My former command, Lenox," Lazarus sobered. "We were ambushed by a full Westphalian GunWall and nearly destroyed. My crew abandoned ship, but I set the vessel on a self-destruct course and escaped into the lifepod that you found, just before destroying it."

"Would your medical records have survived there?" Lenox lifted up a thing that anthropomorphically almost looked like a tiny head with binocular eyes.

Perhaps the better to communicate with certain species.

"Would have, yes," Lazarus agreed. "They are no longer accessible, obviously."

"So noted," the MedCrawler chirped. "I would like to draw a blood sample, and saliva, to help establish a baseline. Could you hold out an arm, please?"

Lazarus did so, and concentrated on maintaining his secrets with a more focused, jaundiced eye. He was starting to have to tell lies to the very people who rescued him, so he would need to be able to keep them straight later.

*Ajax* was destroyed. His lifepod had been shattered, but perhaps there was something there that could be salvaged.

Lazarus was a nobody now, not a former combat captain of the Rio Alliance navy, regardless of what Director Wolcott might think. Or ask of him.

Unless somehow the Innruld ended up being as bad as Westphalia.

Then he might extend his rage to other portions of the galaxy.

# CHAPTER ELEVEN

## ADDISON

DINNER. Addison had agreed with Khyaa'sha that the most bland dinner she could prepare would be a good idea. Bowls of various things cooked with a minimum of spices or oils, with everything normally in them now available in bowls and bottles for the rest of the crew to modify as they liked.

If this Lazarus was truly a former military officer, what other value and experience might he bring?

Per Kuei, the wreckage of his pod had stabilized. The explosion had converted the aft half to a cloud of expanding gas, propelling the forward compartment away with a soft tumble.

Should he put the human to bed in a locked cabin while they went to loot it, or have him up on the bridge, where he might save them from pushing the wrong button?

Dinner would tell.

With so many different methods of locomotion, everyone had a standard spot they normally sat, with Addison at one end and Khyaa'sha at the other, both poised but not using a chair or bench. Or even a nest like Wybert.

Lazarus's legs were too long. He had ended up locating

an aluminum shipping container from the storage compartment to sit on. Hopefully, he had not caught the looks of surprise on so many faces that he could lift nearly one hundred pounds to his chest and just carry it across the deck like it was nothing. The human hadn't even strained or grunted when doing so.

That sort of physical strength was almost frightening.

There would be leftovers, as Addison looked over the bowls. Khyaa'sha had made extra of everything, just so Lazarus had something to eat, once he found it. For now, he had carefully taken a taste of everything, and dipped a number of stirring sticks into the various sauces to dab onto his fat, red tongue. That was the weirdest part of human anatomy, he decided.

And then the human had sat there. Just waiting.

"You are not hungry?" Aileen asked from her space more or less across from Lazarus.

"Famished," he replied with a smile Addison decided was rueful. "However, I'm trying things and waiting to see if any won't stay down. Or poison me. Those six do not taste good to my palette, so I'll assume I cannot digest them. These four are okay. Those three were yummy."

Addison nodded and respected that logic. Who wants to be rescued from sure death in deep space, and then drink alcohol? Well, the human drank some alcohols, but presumably there was a poison out there that would kill him. Hopefully, Khyaa'sha and Lenox had been able to identify which ones were likely and keep them out of dinner.

Addison filled his bowl with noodles and vegetables, adding protein and sauce to make a gourmand quiver with anticipation, but he ate daintily, rather than just upending the bowl into his mouth and making a mess like he really wanted to.

Company. Manners. All that.

The others ate with their usual gusto. Hiring Khyaa'sha as their dedicated cook had been the best thing Addison had done as a director in years.

He studied the human. Lazarus might be the single strongest creature he had ever met at this scale. Innruld were a foot and a half taller, but barely weighed more. Their bodies were as long as their faces, elegant and refined.

They used the lesser species as combat troops and security officers. Workers and servants. Those that didn't flee into the night and sign on with a cargo ship that happened to smuggle things from time to time. Addison smiled and ate slowly.

Lazarus finally took larger samples of the three bowls and ate some. Vegetables, noodles, and the meat of a Galumph. Dumb, slow, and tasty, the furry hexapods were a dietary staple on every planet Addison had ever visited. The sauce was a roasted redfruit that mellowed as you heated it with spices and turned into a good base for many other dishes. If Lazarus could digest it happily, it would make supplies so much easier.

One other weirdness crossed his eyes as he watched. Wybert ate a gruel pudding designed for his kind. Khyaa'sha put some on Lazarus's plate and the human took a dab. It must have been good, from the way his eyes opened suddenly and he sat up straighter.

And then cleaned every bit of it off his plate and into his mouth.

"Close enough, yes," the human said to the cook.

"It serves a similar purpose, and has similar medicinal qualities, Lazarus," Khyaa'sha smiled and went back to her own meal.

Crap, did he have to feed two Ilount now? That stuff was expensive. Still, Lazarus might make it worthwhile.

Everyone settled down to enjoy themselves finally.

"Lazarus, how are you feeling?" Addison asked as Remahle started to clear plates.

The Kr'mari had kitchen duty this week.

"Okay," the human seemed to answer honestly. "At present, everything is digesting, but I have taken a number of prophylactic medicines just in case, so I expect some level of lethargy soon."

Addison took a breath and leapt into the unknown.

"We have been able to locate a portion of your escape pod," he said simply, watching the ripple of electricity that passed through the human. It was almost like seeing a fellow Churquen writhe across hot sands as fast as he could move before he scorched his tail.

"How much?" the human's eyes got big, but at the same time, somehow private.

Must be a biped thing.

"A section of the front," Addison answered him. "The aft was annihilated in the explosion. What was forward that we might salvage?"

"Depends on where the cut is," the human's eye now focused on a spot on a distant wall, near the ceiling. Memory trace. "Engines and star drive aft. Engine room forward from there. Small cargo hold. My quarters, large cabin, kitchen, small quarters, bridge."

"More than a third survived, less than half," Addison envisioned the sleek needle he had seen before, so bizarre to be perfectly symmetrical on the long axis. There were so many more interesting ways to build a ship.

"Maybe right through the kitchen then," Lazarus breathed.

"Why would your quarters be clear at the back, if you were the pilot, Lazarus?" Aileen spoke up, surprising just about everyone at the table. Normally, she was the quiet type who solved three dimensional puzzles to stow cargo in the smallest, most accessible way before going back to her books.

"The ship was actually a courier design," He turned to her and Addison noted the way his voice grew softer and less…something.   Harsh?   Commanding?   Arrogant? Something. "One pilot, hauling some important admiral around, with an aide or two. The engines made noise and needed watching, so the pilot would handle those duties. Made sense to put them aft, when the ship could fly on autopilot."

"Auto-what?" Aileen asked.

"Auto-pilot," Lazarus replied with confusion. "Pre-programmed instructions. How do you handle those tasks?"

"You have not met Cormac, Lazarus," Addison interrupted. "He's our NavCrawler, and handles things when Kuei is off-duty."

"Fully sentient?" Lazarus seemed appalled at the idea. "Isn't that dangerous?"

"He's just another crew member, Lazarus," Addison found his own voice taking on an edge. "Cormac's uptime is measures in decades at this point. Possibly as much as a century."

"Interesting," the human mused. "My kind experimented with such systems early on, but decided against them. We just automate things to dumb computers and then set parameters while retaining oversight."

He paused, studying the sky again.

"But if we cut at midway, then the kitchen might have survived," Lazarus said, turning to Khyaa'sha with a hopeful smile. "All my personal belongings are probably destroyed, so I'll just have to start over."

He seemed to slump in defeat. Addison could understand that.

"Well, it is my plan at present to send Aileen over after

dinner to see what we can salvage," Addison said. "Given your potential medical situation, I would like to have you and Lenox on the bridge with us so you can advise her."

Lazarus wanted to complain. Wanted to volunteer for the duty. Addison could see that in his eyes, even as shrouded as they were. But he also understood that they didn't trust the human.

Not yet, maybe not ever. What bombs or ugly surprises might he work up, if left alone in the wreck? Best to not find out.

"Lazarus of Bethany," he muttered cryptically, but the human nodded, turning to Aileen. "You'll have a camera so I can identify things for you?"

She nodded, still constrained within herself like normal.

Aileen was also the best person he had in zero-gravity. She lived in something similar every time she hit water.

"Good," the human pronounced, turning back to Addison. "How soon do you want to go?"

# CHAPTER TWELVE

## LAZARUS

THERE SHE WAS.

Lazarus stared at the remains of his most recent command with even greater regret than he had encountered putting *Ajax* into her repair orbit and abandoning her until he could return.

The koch still had a slight tumble, but the pilot, Kuei, was in the process of addressing that. She was an Australian kangaroo. Or the closest Lazarus could imagine in space, since her skull was wider, but her face was just as emotive and her eyes didn't seem to miss anything.

Living with aliens, even for a few hours, had given him a much stronger understanding of how non-bipeds approached the concept of clothing. It served two purposes for humans: warmth and pockets.

This ship, this *Shiva Zephyr Glaive* given the constraints of translating across at least two and maybe three languages, was kept at a warmer level than Lazarus had kept *Ajax*. If he was going to be doing anything physical, he would probably leave his jacket shell off and just live in the T-shirt.

Kuei Akeley, like Aileen and Remahle, had fur. Not

much, but it covered her in a thin layer that probably insulated her against all the temperature extremes she might encounter on a spaceship. Her arms were scrawny, like so many of the rest of the crew, but her thighs were bigger than his, almost as large as the tripod tail she rested on at her station.

Over that, she was wearing what Lazarus could only classify as a jumpsuit, sealed up the front, except it didn't have sleeves or legs. A leotard, maybe? Except baggy. And with one big pocket across her stomach where he presumed a pouch, and several more pockets around it.

Standing, she was maybe five feet tall, but those legs and that tail offset her torso and Lazarus figured she weighed at least as much as he did. She did have a smile for him as he intruded onto what she made obvious was her domain, so he trod carefully.

The koch was out there. Part of it. Not really tumbling that much as it drifted across deep space. Lazarus presumed it would eventually enter a cometary orbit, unless the planet that had been nearby when all this started had enough pull to drag it along, or capture it a year from now if it was still here.

The radio came live as Lazarus listened

"Aileen, this is Addison," the Director spoke suddenly, jarring Lazarus.

*The being's name was Addison Wolcott. Director Wolcott, except everyone else called him Addison. Not a familiarity I have earned yet. Perhaps soon. They had been good to me so far.*

"Go ahead, bridge," the Yithadreph woman replied over the comm.

"We're about to capture the hulk," Wolcott said. "Radiation levels are too high to keep it aboard the ship, but you should be fine for now."

The Director clicked something and turned to Lazarus

with slitted eyes that seemed to convey confusion rather than hostility.

"What were you using to power your vessel that would make it that radioactive?" he asked.

"Uranium and thorium in separate generator systems," Lazarus replied. "Not pure-enough uranium to achieve critical mass, but enough to make things hot if it exploded. You could probably wash everything with water if you wanted to and reduce the radiation to much safer levels."

"I don't have the space back there, at present," the director shook his head. "Or the spare water. Maybe we'll push it into a safe orbit somewhere and come back for it later."

Wolcott nodded what looked like thanks and turned his attention to the big screen.

The room wasn't huge, like some of the battleships Lazarus had been on, but it was much roomier than the cabin on the koch, and probably about half the size of *Ajax's* bridge.

The Captain/Director had a chair thingee in the middle of the room, facing the big screen and the physical windows that looked out into space. Kuei was on the starboard side and the NavCrawler Cormac had a docking station to port. There were four other stations facing the wings, two on either side.

"Aileen, stand by," Director Wolcott said from his little hillock throne that he was coiled around and seated atop, just like a Rio Alliance Captain would have done.

"Kuei, all yours."

Lazarus watched the Vaadwig woman—the sentient 'roo —deftly work a series of controls on her board and a golden beam of light suddenly leapt into space. Lazarus didn't remember color, but he'd already been wound a little too tight at that point, wondering if he was about to need his bolter rifle for some ignominious last stand or something.

It grabbed the remains of the koch and stilled the tumble. *Shiva Zephyr Glaive* was already moving at the same pace across the cosmos, so that wasn't difficult, and the dead machine was all of about fifty yards away.

"Aileen, this is Kuei," the Helmswoman said. "We're stable. As you bear."

*As you bear.* In Earth history, that was the order for guns to fire without a central command. Fire when you had your chance.

Here, they were sending a dire otter woman in a spacesuit across the empty gap to try to loot his old ship for supplies, valuables, and hopefully food.

A figure appeared on the screen, floating gracefully across the gap. She didn't land hard on her feet, like Lazarus would have, requiring boot magnets to catch him from bouncing. Instead, all four limbs touched at the same moment and she landed more like a cat. From a pouch, she pulled a net and expanded it out while sticking it to the hull with a magnet of its own.

"About to enter," Aileen said.

Lazarus had given her the codes to the door, but with the back half ripped off, there might not be power for it, and she could just enter the gullet from the aft anyway.

The main screen cut suddenly and Lazarus was looking out from a camera mounted to the top of the woman's helmet. It was always strange doing it this way. You wanted to have them linger on something when they kept moving, or keep moving when they went still.

But she was an expert at this, according to the Director. Probably far more time in a suit than Lazarus had, since most of his time was spent in labs and drydocks.

Down the hull she went and Lazarus had a chance to see

the break. It might have gone right through the refrigerator unit, from the way the hull was torn here. She rounded the corner and her helmet lights punctured the darkness.

Lazarus let go an unconscious sigh of relief.

"Aileen, on your right," Lazarus spoke aloud in as calm a voice as he could manage. "Those two doors are a refrigerator on the bottom and a freezer on the top. Everything inside the freezer is probably fine, but in the lower unit things might have exploded when they froze. Exercise care, or did you want to try to remove the unit as whole and extract it?"

"Bolts to floor and ceiling?" she asked.

"Floor and side wall, across the top, yes," he said.

"We'll take a look at that later," she replied. "Pantry?"

"Latched cupboard doors above the unit and forward," Lazarus said. "There were also some aft."

"Acknowledged," Aileen's voice was more calm than his, but this was just another job to her. "Moving forward."

Lazarus watched her move out of the common space that the kitchen represented and enter into the hallway again. The small quarters were here, a place where one or two aides to an admiral could travel, assuming they required separate quarters.

Not all of the admirals Lazarus had known in his time kept things that discreet.

She opened the door with a magnetic lever she attached, after trying the keypad. Inside, the room was perfectly standard, everything latched down and held in place, just as it had come from the factory, since it had only flown once and Lazarus hadn't slept there. His own cabin would have been far more messy right now, had these folks blown the ship's nose off instead.

Aileen kept up a full running commentary as she went. Lazarus answered questions, but most of what she was seeing was pretty obvious and self-explanatory.

"Moving to the bridge," she said after a few moments.

There.

Lazarus had never seen a ship where the pilot had triggered the ejection system. The top half of the compartment was gone. Both flight seats were gone, although he couldn't remember seeing the second one in his tumbles.

Just the console across the front, with everything duplicated for either pilot to control things if you happened to have two. Things had melted from the heat of the rocket exhaust. Everything had a scorch of some sort, including the carpeting.

"Salvage looks like possibly food, the mechanicals of the refrigerator, and that spare cabin, Addison," Aileen said, turning back an entering the hallway again. "Priorities?"

"How does your unit run?" The Director turned back to Lazarus.

"Alternating electrical current," Lazarus said. "We would need to build a converter from yours, or perhaps an inverter to step it correctly, I would presume. I can advise whoever needs to do that work. There might be instructions written on the back when we remove it."

"Instructions?"

"My mission was military," Lazarus conceded. "And so most of the equipment involved was military as well, so there is a surprising level of bureaucracy involved. Bureaucrats love paperwork."

Wolcott made a sound that reminded Lazarus of a harrumph. Or a suppressed growl.

Nobody ever loves the bureaucrats, until their unbending dedication to paperwork and organization saves the day somehow. Like writing wiring instructions across the back of a refrigeration unit. Lazarus had seen others that way.

"Is there anything of value in that forward cabin, besides aesthetics?" Wolcott continued.

"Negative," Lazarus replied. "Standard issue everything for a junior-ranking officer of no personal importance. All the computer systems were located aft, close to the generators and engines. I suspect at this point the hull has metal value, and that's about it."

"And a semi-galactic civilization has so much metal content available that there's nothing worth considering," the Director completed the thought. "Aileen, see what food you can get from the cupboards first. Then the refrigerator, either to empty, or to remove if you think it might be worth having. Your call."

"Stand by," she said simply.

Lazarus watched her open the first cupboard slowly. They weren't airtight, so everything had bled out, and probably flash frozen, but he could defrost anything that was intact. Most things on a ship were designed for accidental vacuum exposure.

He would just need to make do with what he could get.

# CHAPTER THIRTEEN

## ADDISON

ADDISON HAD NEVER SERVED in a formal navy. The Innruld didn't have such a thing, at least as Lazarus had described his experience, mostly because there were no other independent powers capable of challenging Innruld control of space. Certainly no pitched battles for superiority in a system or trade route.

At least here. This thing called the Rio Alliance, and it's enemy Westphalia, seemed to be rising powers that might threaten the Innruld's grip on this part of the galaxy someday. Especially if all humans were as physically strong as Lazarus appeared to be.

What would a human ship of war be like?

The Innruld had security vessels, but those were just oversized gunboats with the authority to board any vessel and destroy anyone that refused to recognize their authority.

At the other end of the spectrum were smugglers that kept as low a profile as possible while making cargo runs to less-served systems.

Right now, he and several others were starboard aft in the secondary cargo hold, having dragged Aileen's netted catch and Lazarus's bureaucratic refrigerator in through the main airlock and then stashed them here.

The room covered roughly ninety degrees of the curved arc that was the main hull, but only the outer one third of a radius from the edge, with most of the inner portion of that pie slice being the main hold. This was where Addison's crew stored things that were for ship's use, with the occasional overflow when the main hold had too many boxes and tanks of liquid.

Aileen had snagged meals sealed in metal foil containers for stable, long term storage. Spices in a variety of sizes, colors, and apparently flavors, which would make it easier to cook for the human. And maybe expand Khyaa'sha's repertoire. Even a complete set of human silverware that had been sealed up tight in a drawer.

Humans had strange table equipment.

Knives, forks, and spoons in various denominations and scales made sense. He was looking forward to an explanation of the blunt wooden posts that were squared off.

And one refrigerator.

Lazarus had met Ereshkiki Nisab and Thadrakho at dinner. And nerded out with them over Systems Mechanic sorts of things, as only those sort did. Right now, they had the device resting in the middle of several towels and a cargo net in case it did explode upon opening. Aileen had just taped it shut, over the latches already holding it, and shipped it back, on the off-chance that it was insulated enough to hold air and keep the food inside at a reasonable temperature.

The threesome were having a conversation about compressors and regulators, but Addison felt that he should be here, supervising at least in spirit. Ereshkiki Nisab was as close to a second-in-command as this crew needed, but he was frequently keeping engines running and life support pumping oxygen into the ship, so he was a quiet kind of leader.

Thadrakho could fix anything you told him to, but did not go looking for jobs. He wasn't lazy, but Necherle civilization was almost as regulated as Ilount, so his natural default was to expect orders from a superior and act on them immediately and independently.

Still, they made a good team. Lazarus seemed to have enough scientific grounding to explain to the other two what he needed, and Thadrakho was adapting components as he listened.

"So what will we expect inside?" Addison interrupted when the conversation lulled.

"Juice in a frozen concentrate state," Lazarus stood and stretched, reminding Addison how tall the human was. "Dinners prefrozen for heating later in a microwave oven that did not survive. Leftovers in the refrigerator, plus bottles of sauce as condiments, and one container of orange juice that may have exploded from freezing."

"How do we tell?" Addison asked, concerned about liquid leaks on his deck.

"I will run a small video probe into through the door seal," Ereshkiki Nisab rotated on his axis to focus an eye this way. "That will measure pressure and temperature. The machinery itself appears to be intact, and is of a fairly primitive state that relies on mechanical principles instead of electronics we might not have been able to replicate."

Lazarus nodded as he turned to include the Qooph in the conversation. Addison found it amusing that the human reacted to the wheelman with the least surprise, even though he had never encountered the species before. Except he had called it an angel, whatever that was, and laughed at his own joke without explaining it.

Addison stepped back as Ereshkiki Nisab approached the

machine. The Systems Mechanic had added another layer of tape around the unit to keep it from opening, over the tape that Aileen had strapped to it and the handle latch on the front. Instead of a screen, the probe beeped in a code sequence that Addison had a hard time following, but Qooph were primarily an aural-based species.

Lazarus moved to stand next to Addison, lurking over him by nearly a foot, but Addison didn't feel like leaning back and stretching up to look the human in the eyes. It wasn't a dominance stance, as the human had spread his legs to the width of those incredibly-broad shoulders and crossed his wrists behind his back.

It appeared to be an unconscious thing, a trained habit, as he was perfectly parallel to Addison's torso when he stood like this.

Military thing?

"We should be able to salvage things," Ereshkiki Nisab announced after a short symphony played. "The ambient temperature in the large chamber is only a few tens of degrees below freezing, and the pressure is comparable to the ship, although a bit denser. Lazarus, how is our air for you to breathe?"

"Thin," the human said after a beat. "As if I was at a mountainous elevation of perhaps ten thousand feet above sea level on Brasilia. I will acclimate in a few days, but that is why I have been drinking so much water, to keep myself hydrated."

Ten thousand feet? Gods below, his native planet must be a lethal, terrible place, if the gravity was fifteen percent heavier and the atmosphere so thick. No wonder humans were so big and strong. You would need to be to survive such a planet.

Ereshkiki Nisab reached to the door seal with one hand and slid a finger into the seal. He pried it open to create a gap and the air inside whooshed out loudly for a few seconds, chilling the area around it and causing the briefest fog before it warmed and evaporated.

Claw-tipped fingers slit the tape holding the door shut and Ereshkiki Nisab pivoted to bring an eye onto Lazarus.

"It should be safe to open now," the Systems Mechanic said in a five-voice harmony that Addison rarely heard from the man. Only the mouth on the deck had not spoken.

Lazarus moved to the door carefully and grabbed that heavy-looking chromed latch in one meaty hand. He jerked it with his whole upper body and the door opened with a hard pop.

Addison wasn't sure he wouldn't need to coil against something else to achieve that level of lateral torque.

Inside, the containers should have gone every which way, but there appeared to be magnets holding them to the shelves. A useful innovation he might need to discuss with Khyaa'sha at some point.

Nothing had exploded. The orange juice was obvious from the color through the clear container, as was the fact that it had frozen solid and expanded to fill the entire container.

But Lazarus nodded, poked around a little, and closed the door.

"Once you wire it up, Thadrakho, everything will warm to the appropriate temperatures and you should have another space to store things," Lazarus said to the Necherle mechanic.

Thadrakho stood with the power device in his hands and manipulated all four face antennae outwards from those two multifaceted eyes.

"It will be working by morning," it said simply. "Director, where should I place it once it is running adequately?"

Addison leaned back on his coil. The unit was light

enough that anyone could move it on the wheels underneath, once they untelescoped the stands that held it in place. The kitchen upstairs was as filled as geometry would allow. Did he need a refrigerator with cold drinks on the bridge? Or in the engine room?

A plethora of choices.

"Stash it here and out of the way for now," Addison said. "We will address that tomorrow."

He turned to the human. Noted how drawn the face was, with black bags under the bloodshot eyes.

A trying day, but he had not complained more than anyone expected, and less than Addison had been prepared to let slide.

"Let us get you a cabin so you can rest," he said, waiting for Lazarus to nod wearily before setting off.

All the cabins on the main deck were claimed, as well as two of the ones on the upper deck. It would be rude to ask Wybert or Thadrakho to move to an upper bunk to vacate one down here. In the end, Addison had made the decision to put Lazarus in number five upper, inward towards the dead end over the bridge where main sensors were accessed. Remahle would be next to him and Khyaa'sha guarding the end.

Addison led Lazarus to the head and waited while the human did his business. At least the human had some experience with non-humans, and the organic waste systems were intuitively designed.

"You do understand," Addison asked as Lazarus emerged, "that you'll be locked in tonight, and probably for several more as we figure things out?"

It was a measure of tiredness, Addison presumed, that he actually saw the quick flash of anger come across that emotionally-reactive face, for however brief it was. Lazarus's face resumed his normal set, drawn and haggard right now, and kept pace.

"As one might expect," Lazarus replied after a moment. "We are all strangers."

"It will probably be worse when we get to our next destination," Addison kept his face and scales calm as he palmed open the hatch to number five and slithered back out of the way.

"How's that?" Lazarus asked, confusion now layered atop everything else.

"You have no papers from any recognized authority," Addison pointed out. "And I presume, from what you have told me, that simply declaring who you are openly might be something you wished to avoid."

"Absolutely, if possible," the human said. "But Lazarus is not the name I was known by at home. He was a legendary figure who died, and returned to life later. I should be dead at least twice over now, just in the last few days, so I took that name when I decided to survive."

"Then hopefully you have chosen well," Addison imparted as the human stepped into the chamber. "There is an intercom just inside the door if you have needs or problems. Khyaa'sha will monitor it tonight."

"Thank you," Lazarus turned back and said.

Addison could see more words lurking there, but they remained unsaid and the marooned human stepped back into the dimly-lit chamber.

Addison closed the hatch from the outside, locked it, and wondered what he had gotten himself into.

# CHAPTER FOURTEEN



AS CABINS WENT, it wasn't much different that the koch, other than being scaled for someone normally only five feet tall. Lazarus sat down on a bed against the rear wall that was just long enough to pivot and stretch himself out. He would be kicking the bottom in his sleep until he got used to it.

He rose and made his way to what his brain kept wanting to interpret as a makeup mirror, as there was no sink in here, nor a chair. But he supposed everyone would need to bring their own hardware to sit upon.

He would burn that bridge tomorrow.

The crew had made him welcome. More or less.

Wybert had apologized four times for killing the escape pod. Director Wolcott had added two more, and several others had made mention of Wybert's occasionally-comic aggressiveness.

Hopefully, truly an accident.

They had fed him. Treated him like a junior midshipman on his first voyage. Listened to his complaints without crossness.

Smiled. At least as well as their musculature and anatomy allowed.

He stared at the face in the mirror, jumping unconsciously as he recognized something in there.

Lazarus had always stood out among the darker faces and hair of Brasilia, with strawberry-blond hair, green eyes, and what his mother had called Irish freckles covering much of his upper body.

All his friends had been Brasilians going back many generations, while his maternal grandparents had been immigrants. He had been teased mercilessly as a child, and beaten a few times, as such an outsider.

*You don't belong here, gringo.*

Lazarus hadn't been able to refute them, so he'd grown strong. Learned to run when he could and fight when he couldn't. Understood from Papa Michael that it took all kinds and all colors to make the universe work.

In school, he had found his escape with books and science, although looking around at these close walls and seeing the bizarre ship beyond them he shook his head.

His studies had taken him out beyond anything the Rio Alliance had ever told him about. He wondered if they had heard of the Innruld and perhaps never mentioned it to the troops.

Lazarus suspected that the Innruld weren't all that different from Westphalia, at least in politics and specism. From what Aileen and others had said, the cultures shared a similar militant disdain for the *different*. Had the Moah, the Gnashiiley, and the Atomarsk sought out human allies to eventually help them break the Innruld in a future generation when Westphalia was contained?

Conspiracies within conspiracies?

Certainly *Ajax* represented the best of the science of the four species, distilled down into the elegant, lethal functionality of a sword. Just the thing to take apart the previously-overwhelming superiority of the GunWall with a little work and training.

The face that stared back from the mirror now looked a decade older than the one in his cabin aboard *Ajax*, just a week ago. Honed down by stress and exhaustion like one forges a sword by heating and quenching cycles, mixed with the hammer and the anvil.

Lazarus wiped his face with one hand and considered his options.

He was a marooned sailor so far from home he wasn't sure when or even if he could get back to Brasilia. *Ajax* would patiently wait for him, if he could give her the time she needed to repair all the damage Westphalia had inflicted in that terrible ambush.

At the same time, he had gotten the impression from a few words accidentally dropped that this ship was engaged in some sort of criminal enterprise. If so, and they weren't slavers, would they hide him from the Innruld? Or turn him in to them?

Could he be just another anonymous sailor until he figured out where he was and made it back here? Who in their right mind would choose this system to rendezvous with another ship? The planet that had been close by had not given off any radio signals, and there had been no lights visible on the night side.

That smelled an awful lot like two smugglers exchanging illegal cargo in the night, because legitimate sailors would have probably done it dockside, where a customs inspector would have added her stamp to the outside of the box before sending it on its way.

So, criminal underworlds perhaps existed in the realm of the Innruld? Were they universal?

Too much unknown.

Lazarus took off his jacket and laid it flat on the countertop beneath the mirror. He had handled the cool metal of the deck all afternoon in bare feet, but his shoes would have finished hardening by morning so he would be warm enough to just live in the shirt with the brewery logo on the back.

He pulled down the thin blanket from the top of the bed and studied the pillow. Rooting around in the closet, he found two other pillows and added them to the pile so he might sleep.

If that was even an option, as wound up as he was.

At least his stomach had settled. He had taken enough of everything to probably stop a moose, but it had been necessary. With food packs, Khyaa'sha could figure out what he ate and hopefully had enough that he wouldn't have to dose himself silly every meal until he ran out.

Lenox the MedCrawler had studied some of the chemicals, but pronounced himself unable to replicate them with the supplies on hand. Perhaps at the next docking?

Lazarus snorted at the thought of visiting a medical doctor on a station and becoming a whole series of medical journal articles on a new First Contact.

That would raise too many flags. Someone would want to investigate. That would lead to questions about where the human was found.

Which would lead to them asking Director Wolcott why, exactly, this alien was there in the first place.

That might be the single dumbest idea Lazarus had heard in years, but he could not fault the robot for the linear thinking that got it there. Lenox was trying to treat a new organic, and doing the best it could.

Lazarus laid down and shook his head. The lights were just bright enough that he could see the room, but in his chest, that heart was banging a bass drum as fast as it could.

Maybe if he could meditate a little and relax, he would be able to sleep.

Then his eyes closed and exhaustion pulled him into the depths.

# CHAPTER FIFTEEN

## LAZARUS

MORNING.

Lazarus came back to the universe from someplace far away. Dark and foreboding. His personal clock was messed up and there wasn't an electronic one in here on the dresser, so he was just floating in darkness. At least it was warm.

The smells of yesterday seemed to have fully faded. It was always like that when you boarded a new ship. He had been expecting it to last longer because he was dealing with more than just human scents in the air, but maybe his nose was as tired as he felt.

Except he wasn't tired. He felt rejuvenated almost.

Lazarus lifted a hand from the bunk and his brain finally engaged. Light gravity. Only about eighty percent of Brasilia or *Ajax*. He had been sleeping on a cloud, even as his mind had descended into hell and dueled with Cerberus for passage.

He laughed and sat up.

"Lazarus, are you awake?" the voice of an angel descended on him.

Intercom. Light. Clock, too, over there under the

intercomm when he looked. Early morning, if he was mathing correctly. Not a sure bet.

"I am," he replied as the tones became Khyaa'sha.

A more unlikely angel he had a hard time imagining, but didn't every angel descend with "Fear not, human," before they imparted their message, as they were so alien that primitive minds could not understand that the strange creature they beheld was a messenger from God?

Had the Qooph visited Earth in some magnificently ancient era and spoken to Ezekiel? Certainly the description of that angel was close, although the Systems Mechanic here only rolled on one axis at a time, rather than all.

Or had a Qooph in a hardshelled environment suit traveled on Bronze Age Earth inside a sphere so that he could turn any direction as necessary?

He would not ask Ereshkiki Nisab today, but it might be worth researching the species' astronomical history someday, to see if they had perhaps made it as far as Earth four or five thousand years ago.

"Are you ready to face your second day?" Khyaa'sha asked with a lilt in her voice that was friendly and concerned, while still being alien.

But then, they were just people. Lazarus was the alien here, wasn't he?

"I am." Lazarus swung his legs off the bunk and stood, careful not to leap into the air and bash his head. The ceilings on this ship tended to either be seven feet or fourteen, depending. Lower than he was ready for.

Everything was just enough off to leave him gasping from time to time, and the thin air didn't help.

He heard the door unlatch and he stretched to loosen all the kinks from sleeping curled up on his side in a bed too short.

Goldilocks with freckles.

"The others should be stirring soon," Khyaa'sha said. "Does your kind bathe in running water?"

Bathe in running water? Oh. Shower.

"Yes," Lazarus said. "Shower is the term I am familiar with."

"Addison showed them to you last night?" she asked. "Red for hot. Green for cold."

"Indeed," Lazarus replied. "Where would I find a towel to dry myself?"

"In the bottom drawer under the mirror," Khyaa'sha said. "I shall look for you in a bit. There is something I wanted to prepare for you this morning that I think will serve your immediate nutritional needs."

Because sure, a giant pinwheel spider woman fixing you breakfast was the most normal thing in the galaxy, wasn't it?

Lazarus found the towel. A bottle of general detergent had been recovered from the koch, so he could get himself clean, if a little raw, at least until he found something less harsh. Or shaved his head and kept everything so short that he didn't need to wash it.

He ran a hand over his chin and felt the first hint of bristles. It was another thing that marked him separate from the others back home, how slow his ginger-colored beard grew. Some of his friends in college had needed to shave twice a day, while he needed to skip several days before his beard even started to be visible.

But he would need to find or fashion a razor soon. Maybe Thadrakho could build him something? The man had a knack for that sort of work, what Papa Michael called *rednecking*.

Towel over his shoulder like he was back at the Merchant Marine Academy, Lazarus opened the hatch and turned left. Past two cabins he stopped first at the head and then entered the thing his mind kept wanting to refer to as the "Shower Event."

The room was twenty feet long and ten wide, with high ceilings that Lazarus could only touch if he jumped in the low gravity to the extreme of his muscles. It wasn't tiled like it would be back home, but there were shower heads at all heights and directions, each with perhaps a dozen options one could dial in to adjust flow, pressure, and pattern as you needed.

Lazarus picked the highest head, the one he presumed was normally used by Thadrakho, as the only person here taller than Lazarus, not counting Wybert's overall horizontal length. He stripped and stashed his clothes well away so they would remain dry and entered the combat arena.

Hot was really hot, he discovered fast enough, nearly scalding his hand. *Ajax* had never had enough time in the tanks to heat the water, so hot always came out mostly a little better than warm, unless he timed his showers to the dead of night or the middle of a watch. Someone here liked really hot showers.

Once the temperature was low enough to be comfortable, Lazarus just stood under the water and let it wash yesterday off of him. All of yesterdays.

Everyone before *Lazarus*.

He wasn't sure how long he stood there, unconsciously expecting the timer to kick in and cut the water flow, like back at the Academy when you didn't want students spending their days in there.

A voice intruded and Lazarus opened his eyes like a shot.

"What kind of claws do you have?" the voice broke his concentration.

Lazarus looked over in a near panic and realized that Aileen was naked and showering next to him, looking up at him expectantly with those deep, dark eyes.

He had never showered with a female. Barracks and warships always had male and female showers port and starboard, along with cabins separated by gender down the centerline.

You didn't necessarily do that on a civilian ship. Or an alien one where females outnumbered males, if he had done the math right yesterday.

Four foot six. Covered with a thick fur of short bristles. Expressive eyes. Wide mouth. Ambulatory whiskers and ears.

And breasts. Covered over with fur except for reddish-gray nipples that were visible.

Lazarus's mind simply descended into white noise.

"You awake?" she snapped at him.

"Maybe," he opened his eyes again, but there was still a naked Yithadreph woman soaping herself, all of four feet away.

"What kind of claws do you have?" she repeated herself with a little exasperation.

Lazarus held out a hand, unable to even parse her syntax into something that made sense. She took it in both of hers, hands with four fingers and an opposable thumb, all rather stubby and webbed compared to his. And covered over with finer fur.

She ran a thumb over the ends of his fingers and inspected them by pulling him closer. Lazarus didn't have anything left with which to resist her, even as strong as he normally was.

Her shower was not running much hotter than his, from where she pulled his arm into it.

"I need a scratch," she said, looking up at him with serious eyes. "Remahle's kind don't have good claws to dig in, but you might. And I'm not limber enough to reach my spine with any good leverage."

Yup. White noise.

Lazarus finally found coherence. He was showering with a woman, alien though she might be, and she wanted him to soap and scratch the fur along her spine, all the way down to the cute stub of a tail sticking out.

Hoping that his day had already reached its weirdest point, and that everything else was downhill from here, Lazarus took the bar of what he assumed was soap from her paw and lathered up his hands. He considered it, found the idea acceptable, and dropped down to his knees next to Aileen, where they were almost of a height.

"Turn around," he managed when she looked back at him in surprise.

She did. He soaped up her back with the bar before resting it on the wet floor and proceeded to sink his nails into the fur and work the soap in.

In his mind, it didn't feel that much different from the German Shepherd his family had had when he was much younger. Bristly fur. Oils that came off. A body that backed into his fingers as he found the right pressure and rhythm.

If she'd been a cat, he might have expected her to purr after a bit.

"Okay, that was good," she stepped away from him. "Stand up and I'll do you now."

Lazarus let that comment go at face value and levered himself back to his feet. Aileen had similar claws to a human, once she got to work on his back, even if she had to stand on her toes to get higher than his shoulder blades.

The soap had a nice smell. Clean, instead of the industrial chemical taint of the stuff he had brought from the ship. But that was for plates, not humans.

And a good back scratch really made all the difference in the world, facing his day.

She finished and stepped back.

"Thank you," he said, turning to finish rinsing and then shutting his water off.

It was just the most natural thing in the world, right? Showering with an alien woman who needed you to soap and scratch her back.

Perfectly sane.

He dried himself off and got dressed, unable to keep from stealing glances at her. Short legs and arms, compared to a human. Long torso. A ridge of fur about three fingers wide right down the center of her spine, which was why having help grooming was so important.

As xenobiology went, Lazarus had seen weirder. From a safe distance. In a nature documentary vid.

He finished dressing as Aileen shut off her shower so he decided to retreat rather than ogle the Yithadreph woman as she did the same.

Outside, the smell of something drew him past the food storage compartment and into the kitchen area. The tables out here were empty as yet, so perhaps the others had not risen. It was early in the ship's day, and Lazarus had gotten the impression that Director Wolcott had intended to stay up later doing something after he put the human to bed.

Khyaa'sha looked up from her pot and smiled at him. He hoped it was a smile. The two big mandibles opened and clacked, and her eyes got big for a second.

"Ah, right on time," she said, pivoting from where she was resting back on her abdomen and six legs to take a ladle and pour something into a bowl. There was no steam, so it wasn't oatmeal. Hot oatmeal, anyway. "Try this."

He took it and she turned back to her kitchen, purring or perhaps humming to herself as she worked.

Lazarus took the low bowl and made his way back to the tables overlooking the main cargo hold. Pure water came from a nozzle next to the glasses, so he took two trips getting everything to where his shipping container still waited.

Aileen joined him about the time Lazarus finally got organized enough to study the bowl. Thicker than soup. Smoother than oatmeal.

Pudding? It had the color of butterscotch.

Aileen was eating something that looked like a cooked salad and largely ignoring him, so he took up a spoon and took a dab.

Sniffed it.

Considered.

Sweet, but rather earthy. Cardamom and brown sugar kind of smell.

He took the briefest taste. Yes. Sweetness. Brownness. Milkiness. Maybe start with coconut cream and flatten the taste out with nutmeg and brown sugar and allspice.

After a moment, his brain finally engaged. This was Wybert's gruel, but modified. Cut, maybe, with a different set of spices and fluids from what the Ilount had been eating last night.

Lazarus really felt inspired to locate coffee. Director Wolcott's crew had something similar in taste, but the plant from which it was derived didn't have any caffeine in it.

And he really needed something to bring him alive this morning.

Clacking on the deck indicated Wybert's arrival. Nothing else made as much noise as a decapeed. Lazarus considered suggesting booties with a soft, rubber sole, so he could still grip, but didn't necessarily tell everyone in the neighborhood who was arriving.

An antenna appeared over his right shoulder right next to his ear, along with a blueish skull. The outer left eye stared at Lazarus and blinked, and the four mandibles clacked once.

"That smells good," Wybert said, leaning a little weight on the back of Lazarus's shoulder.

He hoped that Ilount didn't drool. Or if they that did it wasn't caustic.

"Khyaa'sha's trying something for me this morning," Lazarus replied without screaming or leaping into the air once. "I think she made you some."

"Goodie," and he was gone.

Lazarus remembered to breathe. Aileen snickered so quietly that nobody but him would hear it. He studied her and saw the wry grin pulling her whiskers and lips to the right. Today, the Capri pants she was wearing were gray, and the vest a soft maroon not that different from the pants he was stuck with back in his cabin until he found or made something else.

"He can be a dork," she announced. Like that might be a trade secret.

Lazarus shrugged and took a larger taste from the bowl. Almost butterscotch pudding, if he added something. Might need to break out all the spices Aileen had rescued and see what worked. It went down smooth and seemed to have the same jolt of energy he got from honey.

Hopefully, some of the antibiotic qualities that the Ilount found would work here as well. There had to be all manner of alien germs and bugs floating around.

Director Wolcott appeared about the time Lazarus was finished scraping the bowl clean and lamenting that he didn't have a prehensile tongue with which to get the last bits.

That was good. He almost felt like he wanted to survive this morning, but for the lack of coffee.

"Good, you have eaten," Wolcott announced. "How is your medical condition?"

*My what? Ah, bad translation into a second language.*

"I'm good this morning," Lazarus replied. "What can I

do to start earning my keep?"

"Muscles when we dock, but I would like you to join me on the bridge, if you would."

Lazarus rose and bussed everything into the appropriate bin before following the Director down the ramp and forward.

Kuei was on the bridge, along with Cormac the NavCrawler, when they arrived. Out the big window everything was a pearlescent gray shot through with the strangest blues.

Lazarus was entranced.

"So we are currently in trans-space," the Director stated. "Making our way out of this system and back to safe space. What path did you use to get into this pocket?"

"In trans-space?" Lazarus felt his jaw drop open. "*In?*"

"Yes," Wolcott turned his entire being on a coil and stared at Lazarus. "Is this not how you travel FTL?"

Lazarus felt the bottom of the universe fall out from under him. Actually traveling through FTL space slow enough that you could measure it? *Ajax* used star drives. Hell, everyone used them.

Aim yourself at a destination by calculating right ascension, declination, and distance. Punch an instant hole between the two and arrive as close as your sensors, calculations, and gravity deflections would allow.

But to actually travel through some sort of alternate universe at trans-light speeds?

"Lazarus?" Wolcott asked.

Lazarus opened his mouth and nothing came out. On top of the immense firepower of *Ajax*, what would a star drive be worth to a culture that had to travel slowly through FTL space?

"I don't know," Lazarus finally stammered, trying to keep the panic in his voice to just being lost and shot down and rescued by aliens. Nothing about apparently descending from a more-advanced technological culture than the one he had found himself in.

Even the light gravity overcame him and Lazarus found himself sitting on his butt on the cold deck, hoping the room would stop spinning.

"Lenox to the bridge immediately!" Lazarus heard a voice yell. "Emergency."

His own heart was suddenly pounding a triphammer beat so fast he thought his head might explode.

Wolcott appeared in his field of vision.

"Can you hear me?" the naga-man appeared to be yelling.

"Yes," Lazarus managed. "Sorry."

The words seemed to cause the tides of madness to suddenly recede. Lazarus looked at his hands, and they were fluttering, but he could clench them. Move them.

Standing right now sounded a little stupid, but the deck was doing a capital job of holding him up, so he stayed still and let it.

The MedCrawler had appeared and was shining a sensor at him.

"Are you well, Lazarus?" Lenox asked.

"I think so," he replied.

"What was that?" Wolcott asked.

"Stress, I think," Lazarus replied. "All of the everything just boiled over on me and my body had a reaction. I should be better."

Kuei, of all people, helped him to his feet, but she was a muscular tripod, so she could do that.

"So how did you manage to find this space?" Wolcott asked in a quieter tone.

"Luck," Lazarus said with complete honesty. "My ship was already coming apart, so I got into the boat as she did.

As the captain, I was the last person aboard, the others having escaped at the end of the battle to be captured. I was intent on destroying *Ajax*, so I blasted clear on a random course designed to destroy the vessel. Once that was done, I took the koch."

He knew he was rambling, but Lazarus had given it much thought yesterday and this morning to his story, and what he was saying was generally close enough to the truth that he wouldn't trip himself up with a lie later.

"So you don't know where the wreckage of your ship ended up?" Wolcott asked, obviously interested in the possibility of salvage.

"The information was stored in the koch," Lazarus said. "In the computers that were located aft before they were destroyed."

"Pity, but just as well," Wolcott mused. "You will be interesting enough to explain to authorities as an unknown alien species. Your ship might have caused the Innruld to get involved."

"They don't care about aliens like me?" Lazarus was amazed.

"Oh, they care, but only so far as they need to classify you and make sure you aren't bringing any diseases aboard a ship or station, and their flunkies will handle that task," the Director smiled. "Lenox will provide them those records."

"And what cover story will you use for me?" Lazarus asked.

"A variant of the truth." Wolcott seemed to relax now. "Shipwrecked sailor of unknown type. Possibly an explorer, possibly a runaway from some other ship, since you know Innruld well enough already. If we blame some other ship for failing to report you, perhaps one crewed entirely by Kuei's kind, that should cause suspicion to fall elsewhere."

"That's mean," the Helmswoman spoke up suddenly.

"She has it coming, Kuei," Wolcott looked over as he snapped. "For a variety of reasons."

"True, but setting the Innruld on her won't make her happy."

"And she dare not do anything about it without confirming non-existent suppositions on the part of our overlords," Wolcott sounded cruel now. "Thus causing them to spend even more time going over her records and history. I win either way."

Lazarus didn't feel like asking, but could smell the bad blood. Must be old rivals or friends of Kuei Akeley. Perhaps former crewmates who had done her and Director Wolcott wrong at some point?

And they traveled at an FTL speed through some sort of alternate universe they called trans-space. Thank God nobody had apparently understood the flash of blue light when the koch jumped.

Now he really needed to keep *Ajax* hidden and secret until he could steal a ship and return here. The Innruld sounded almost as bad as Westphalia, or he might consider giving them a tech upgrade and aiming them at Earth.

Better to overthrow both and let the galaxy right itself afterwards. He had never imagined how many intelligent species there must be out here.

Lenox insisted on a checkup aft where he had extra equipment, so the conversation with Wolcott was cut short, but that just meant fewer lies right now while he processed what story he could tell them.

If he told them anything more.

He owed them for the rescue, but interstellar law supposedly *required* a ship to stop and assist other ships and marooned sailors. Ethics as well.

He would see just how far that would carry them.

Or him.

# CHAPTER SIXTEEN

## ADDISON

ADDISON SAT IN HIS OFFICE, just aft of the bridge next to the primary escape pod. They would be another day getting clear of the nebula and pivoting back to Innruld space for the run to Dormell. He had time to come up with a good story to cover his extra crewmember, since he wasn't supposed to even be in the Phraettis Nebula in the first place.

It was Lazarus that concerned him. Perhaps the human had an emotional overload moment, but the concept of FTL had been what set him off in the first place.

How in the Six Hells did humans cross trans-space? Most of the area beyond the nebula was unknown and unexplored. Did the humans come from that direction? That he knew the Moah and the Gnashiiley lent credence to the theory. The Atomarsk worlds were supposedly so far away that they were just legends in these sectors of space, but the other two were species one might encounter if you went far enough.

But Addison was sure that the human didn't cross trans-space the same way as *Shiva Zephyr Glaive*. How the hell did he do it? What secrets had been lost?

Now, more than ever, Wybert's casual mistake in

destroying that tiny ship weighed heavily. Had Addison lost the opportunity to break the Innruld's hold over the other species?

Worse, should he come clean with Lazarus about his true purpose and enlist the human's help? Load up the ship with supplies and try to locate the human homeworlds so he could buy or steal their technology if it was better?

The trade routes he might open would pay for such a voyage all by itself, but Addison had no interest in making the Innruld overlords even more wealthy than they were now. Or letting them take over such trade.

No, those eight containers aft would do enough damage to Innruld society. Who could have imagined that a simple weed that grew by the side of the road on a Vaadwig world could be refined into an intoxicant so perfectly designed to trap the more weak-minded of the Innruld into a narcotic dependence severe enough to disrupt lives and families?

*Perhaps, dear overlords, if you had not subjugated the rest of us, we wouldn't be so interested in destroying you? Wouldn't go moving heaven and earth for the tools to overthrow you from the inside out?*

*Wouldn't consider asking a human what weapons his kind might have that could break the Innruld forever?*

Because he had seen it in Lazarus's eyes, right before the madness hit. Culture shock, but more importantly, *technology shock.*

Addison keyed the comm to the engine room.

"Ereshkiki Nisab, could you join me in my office, please?" Addison asked when the Qooph answered.

"Momentarily," the being replied before cutting the circuit.

Addison meditated on the issue, but no solution presented itself. Worse, was the human a spy sent to determine their own technology before invading? Was that species so far advanced that they could simply step in and replace the overlords with their own cruelties, whatever those might be?

The ancient tale of the djinn would not leave his mind. A powerful, magical spirit trapped in a bottle. If you released him, he might grant you four wishes, and he might just decide to destroy you instead.

The hatch slid aside and Addison's Systems Mechanic entered, coming to rest by deflating one of his roller sacks to plant a hex-side on the deck.

"What troubles you, Addison Wolcott?" the Qooph asked, quietly. Only three voices spoke.

Addison closed the hatch and locked it before he spoke.

"I had the human, Lazarus, on the bridge earlier," Addison replied. "He seemed shocked and surprised that the ship was in trans-space. *In*. That seemed a foreign concept to him."

"Most interesting," Ereshkiki Nisab answered. "Did he clarify how humans did it?"

"He did not," Addison said. "In fact, he had a medical incident in response. He put it down to overall shock, but I wonder."

"How else would they cross the depths of space?" the Systems Mechanic probed.

"I leave that to your speculation and writers of the fantastical," Addison replied. "I am more interested in the other half of his story. He said his ship was nearly destroyed and he abandoned it into the smaller ship we did destroy before it went. But he was also confused when I asked which of the few pathways into the nebula he had flown. As if he had not needed one of the secret trails."

"Interesting, indeed," the wheelman rocked side to side a little on his rims, a thing he did when he was deep in thought.

"I would ask you to consult your old records when you have a chance, Ereshkiki Nisab," Addison said. "Yours is the eldest of the star-faring races. Is there perhaps another way to travel other than through trans-space? And have your kind ever encountered humans in your wanderings before the Innruld rose in conquest?"

"I have had the same thoughts, Addison Wolcott," the Qooph stopped rocking and one eye focused hard in his face. "When we reach Dormell I will pass a message along to the Elders of the Wide Road to tap their wisdom. It is possible that some memory of Lazarus's kind remains."

"Good, my friend," Addison continued. "The other conundrum is whether or not we should seek the human worlds ourselves for the trade and technological potential. Can we keep such a thing secret? Or is the human a spy sent among us as a prelude to conquest? Lazarus has mentioned great battles in space between large groups of warships. The Innruld have nothing like that at present."

"There are none that could challenge them," Ereshkiki Nisab said.

"Exactly," Addison agreed. "But what if there was such a threat? What if the humans could take the overlords down?"

"Would they free us, or just replace our masters?" Ereshkiki Nisab asked.

"Or even seek to eliminate us, as Lazarus claims would be the policy of Westphalia," Addison replied. "Not just subjugating our worlds, but clearing them for human colonization."

"This is why you are a much better Director than I could ever be, Addison Wolcott," the Qooph laughed with at least two mouths as he spoke with others. "Even with six eyes, I cannot see the various twists and turns as well as you can. Do we ask the human or does that risk alerting him to our suspicions?"

"We watch," Addison said. "We take him to Dormell and perhaps allow him to continue to fly with us. Or to seek alternate transport home, if that is his goal. We can always alert the Innruld and let them take him into custody if he does seem to be a spy, but that option burns all the others. At least until we know his heart."

"Did he not say that he had taken a new name with the rebirth of surviving that battle?" Ereshkiki Nisab asked. "Become a new person in some ethical and moral mechanism?"

"He did," Addison answered.

"And you have not yet seen enough to judge?"

"*In the heat of anger, the truth emerges*," Addison quoted the old maxim. "Hopefully our human will be well enough to be additionally stressed before Dormell, Ereshkiki Nisab. I would have his truth."

"Or his soul?"

"Better his than ours, Ereshkiki Nisab," Addison replied. "Especially with the secrets that you and I carry."

# CHAPTER SEVENTEEN

## LAZARUS

HE HAD BEEN CLEARED for duty but Lazarus was only physically well. His mind still could not grasp some sort of hyperspatial transit capability that was slow enough to notice. How did you see to steer? Or did you?

Too much to learn, but he dared not tell Director Wolcott the depths of his ignorance without revealing the tremendous technological leap forward that star drives represented. To arrive somewhere in between blinks of an atomic clock instead of sailing like the old-fashioned thruster-cruisers that humans had used within their system before the first Atomarsk ships suddenly appeared overhead?

It had taken centuries before the star drives were born. Had that technology never made it beyond the Rio Alliance and Westphalia?

So much to learn. From the stories over breakfast and dinner last night, the nebula that was supposed to have been his grave apparently separated zones of the galaxy similar to how the oceans had once done on Earth. Stars so densely packed that *Ajax* should have hit one.

*Shiva Zephyr Glaive* was apparently cautiously feeling her

way out through one of several secret trails. He almost felt like Leonidas at Thermopylae, wondering when the Persians might emerge from the hills to fall on his back.

At least Director Wolcott was some level of criminal, with no love for the Innruld. Lazarus might have time to plan a way home. Or steal a ship and long-sail it across the intervening thousand light-years if he could.

Today, Aileen had him restacking boxes in the main cargo hold to make things more efficient. It was hard work, but apparently he had twice the upper body strength of anyone else on the crew. That made sense, considering he shared this atmosphere with a Churquen, a Qooph, a Vaadwig, a Yithadreph, a Kr'mari, a Tarni, an Ilount, a Necherle, and two Crawlers.

Didn't most jokes start that way? Perhaps with a bar and a traveling salesman thrown in for good measure?

He could do this. Pick up a box two feet cubed and lurch from one stack to another as she marked things on a checklist. The occasional awe he saw in her eyes told him how hard this would have been for everyone else to do. The crates tended to run fifty to one hundred pounds, with the ones heavier than that marked in purple.

Those he would do with a powered handtruck not all that different from the kind *Ajax* carried. Physics was physics, after all. Slide a pair of forks under a wooden pallet, or grip something by the sides if it was on the deck directly. Pump up the hydraulics to lift it. Drag it around by dead weight.

Even on wheels, some of these weighed more than he did, and the deck had a rough pattern raised to induce friction, so he couldn't just squat down and slide them across the floor easily.

Lazarus knew he would pay for this level of manual labor later, but there were more than one hundred containers in here, mostly one-or two-foot boxes, plus a set of standard cylindrical tanks about a foot across and four feet tall. The colors of the metal apparently had nothing to do with the contents, so he had to look closely at the labels attached and occasionally sound things out phonetically before he touched them.

Aileen seemed to appreciate his care and patience with those as well, which told him how explosive some of them must be.

He took the current box and stacked it three high in a corner, in a place where the rest of the crew might need an overhead crane to get it down later. But doing things this way also opened up a lot of space if they could use the corners more effectively to move things around.

"That's that," Aileen said, checking the last item off her list. "Inspectors at Dormell will be able to look directly at the containers we're off-loading and depart that much faster. Thank you. It would have taken me at least another two days, and we have added up almost twenty percent volume capacity using the space under the catwalks like this."

"You're most welcome," Lazarus said with a little bit of a gasp. "Now what?"

"This was supposed to take all day today and most of tomorrow, so I suppose a break for now," Aileen said. "You can always mop up some more decking, unless you're ready to learn vehicle maintenance from Wybert or work on electrical or hydraulic tasks under Ereshkiki Nisab."

"Yes, a break would be better," Lazarus said. "Does the ship have a library? I would like to learn anything about where we're going. I didn't even know Innruld space existed two days ago."

She got nervous. Twitchy, even. Eyed him sidelong for several moments. Not quite enough to make him nervous, but Lazarus wondered what minefield he had just wandered into.

"You read Innruld?" she finally asked in a low, quiet tone.

"Interlac," he corrected her. "They appear to be close enough in the written form that they are the same language, or were at one point. Mandarin and Cantonese, as it were."

Blank look. Non-human who has never heard of Beijing or Hong Kong.

"Two languages on the human homeworld," he tried to explain. "Both evolved regionally from a common verbal ancestor in distant history and share the same written form."

She nodded, still confused, but perhaps in a different direction now.

"You don't have a reader," she said simply.

"I have nothing but the clothes on my back," Lazarus nodded back at her, reminding her how he came to be here.

"I have a few books you might borrow to read," she said so quietly Lazarus wasn't actually sure she had spoken.

And she appeared to blush as she did. Weird.

Apparently the day intended to keep getting more strange instead of less.

"Thank you," he said.

"Follow me," Aileen ordered.

Lazarus wiped his dirty hands on his pants and made a note to ask about doing laundry soon, as well as finding more clothing, although he expected he would have to make something for himself given the proportions around here. And the lack of bipeds in much of the crew.

Her cabin was the middle of the five small ones on the main deck, Director Wolcott apparently having a double closest to the bridge. As Lazarus had surmised earlier, the ship had been heavily modified to include a shallow pool about seven feet across and maybe eighteen inches deep, on a raised platform with a lip and a drain.

Lazarus blushed to himself as he realized that Aileen probably slept nude while floating, much like the Terran otter she resembled. But he'd already seen her nude. Scrubbed her back in the shower.

*Let's just pile up the weirdness with some frosting.*

Aileen left the hatch open as she entered, but he stayed back at the threshold, leaning against the frame. Her cabin was otherwise like his, with the addition of a metal bookcase in one corner where he had coathooks emerging from the wall. And clothes hung from the back of a chair and what looked like a vest tossed on the floor having missed what his brain interpreted as a laundry hamper. Thirty or forty volumes of books caught his eye, from slender to thick and apparently bound with cloth rather than leather, across a spectrum, but mostly in black.

She turned when she realized he was staying outside of her space. Frowned for a second and then smiled discreetly.

"Innruld history?" she asked simply.

"Whatever you have that would put me in the best position to answer questions when the authorities ask," Lazarus said. "Or to tell the best lies if Director Wolcott needs that from me."

"Why would he need you to lie?" she asked defensively, turning more to face him in surprise.

"Whatever rendezvous you had out here in the middle of nowhere needed secrecy," he smiled grimly. "If it was legitimate cargo, you could have done it on a dock somewhere, or in orbit of an inhabited planet. That you had to sneak out here suggests that I might need to be completely clueless about where you picked me up, so nobody could backtrack you. Close?"

"Too close," she said in a serious tone. "You're smarter than you let on."

"I was a Director on another ship, like Wolcott," he said,

feeling his back come up just a little. "Moreso, because that was a warship with a crew of one hundred, and not just a cargo trader. You didn't grasp that?"

"I didn't," she admitted harshly, grabbing a book from the shelf and starting his way. "You'll need this initially, but we need to talk to Addison about what else you should know."

Lazarus let her stuff the tome into his hands as he stepped back out of her way. She blew right past him and headed forward so he fell into her wake and walked slow enough that he didn't run into the Yithadreph woman when she stopped.

They found Kuei and Cormac on the bridge when the hatch opened.

"Where's Addison?" Aileen asked bluntly.

"Office," Kuei looked up from her game, or whatever she was doing on the screen.

Didn't look like piloting.

Aileen pivoted right under his hip and turned to the left hand door on the aft of the ship's head, rapping on the metal.

The door opened a moment later, revealing Director Wolcott behind a medium-sized metal desk, and the Qooph, Ereshkiki Nisab, on this side, resting on a flat. He pivoted to turn a critical eye on Lazarus, standing above and behind Aileen as she took a breath.

"I suggest you two need to chat more with Lazarus," she said simply. "Now, before he reads too much Innruld history in the book I gave him."

She turned and lit out like Lazarus might be chasing her, moving as rapidly as those stubby legs might carry her away from him.

Lazarus stood in the door and composed his face.

"Come in," Wolcott said. "We were just talking about you."

Lazarus understood the Qooph to be the other officer on this crew, with the rest really just being enlisted sailors, although there was no rank structure here. Each crewmember had specialties, and he had been attached to Aileen Enjehn because she was the person best at packing and understanding cargo containers, just as Thadrakho was good at repairing things and Wybert understood combat.

Lazarus entered the Lion's Den remembering Sunday School lessons of Daniel.

"I surprised Aileen," he said simply. "Pointed out to her that I felt I should learn more about the Innruld, in case I needed to tell convincing lies to the authorities when they interrogated me."

"What deceptions do you foresee, Lazarus?" Ereshkiki Nisab asked in that awesomely bizarre harmony you could achieve with several mouths speaking at once.

He could see why Ezekiel might have believed God had sent such a creature.

"I am an ignorant sailor rescued by Director Wolcott and the crew of *Shiva Zephyr Glaive*," Lazarus leaned back against the wall to relax, since there was no chair that would fit him until he grabbed himself a box or made something. "But they'll ask where I was found, and I suspect that telling them about that hollow space in the nebula would be counter-productive to your business and perhaps a vast number of your associates."

Both men froze. Beings. Creatures.

People. They were people. Leave it at that and don't try to understand why God chose so many interesting shapes for His children.

But the two people had been caught with hands in cookie jars, however metaphorically.

Lazarus nodded.

"Smugglers?" he guessed, watching Addison Wolcott for

subtle cues, since he had no idea how to read the body language of a four-foot-tall blue-gray wheel with two rims, two arms, six eyes, and six mouths.

Not yet, anyway. The hands and eyes probably told you things, once you paid enough attention.

Lazarus had no idea if they might kill him now. If the secrets these two kept were worth more than his life. But he also owed them one of his lives. And if they were nice enough, and the Innruld as bad as everyone here seemed to think, then perhaps he might need to take *Ajax* on a slight detour before he headed home.

"Are you truly a rebel, Lazarus?" Wolcott asked.

"The Rio Alliance considers itself an independent, stellar nation," he replied. "Westphalia disputes that notion and seeks to dominate every world they cannot conquer. Your kind would be distinctly unwelcome. They would classify me as a rebel. I'm just a scientist with a military background, but yes, I certainly plan on making sure that someone sticks it to Westphalia in the most painful way possible."

"Then perhaps you understand my relationship with the Innruld after all," Wolcott smiled. "None of the other species are free from their dominance. You will not be, either, but if you are too stupid to even know your homeworld's coordinates, then there is not much they can do to bother other humans."

"Perhaps, old friend, they already know humans?" Ereshkiki Nisab spoke up, glancing the topmost of those big eyes over at Wolcott for a second. "Who is privy to the inner councils of the Innruld? Lazarus, from which direction did you enter the nebula?"

"Trailing and farther out on the rim," Lazarus decided to give them that much truth.

Westphalia would not welcome even more aliens,

whereas the Rio Alliance most certainly would, if they showed up.

"From my homeworlds, the nebula appears as a wide, flat shield across several degrees of sky," Lazarus continued. "I still don't know how I managed to get in there without hitting something."

"If you did, that suggests a straight enough path from your worlds," Wolcott said. "And an unknown one, because all the paths I know hook significantly around star systems. But that is not today's task."

"Indeed," Lazarus agreed. "What do I tell people?"

"I think if you tell them the wrecked and destroyed spaceship story, that will be sufficient," Ereshkiki Nisab replied instead of Wolcott. "It would not be to your long-term interest to mention that it was a warship, or that you commanded such a vessel. You should fall back on the common caricature of the erect biped as a simple dupe from the lower decks who has never even met his previous captain, let alone stood on the bridge of your previous vessel. Addison and I can deflect everything from that point, and your ignorance on the topic will not haunt any of us. Is this satisfactory?"

"It is," Lazarus decided. "What should I tell Aileen or the others?"

"That much, and little more," Addison Wolcott said. "We will tell the crew what they need to know. If they know little, they cannot accidentally tell anyone. Perhaps you should refrain from discussing your past with anyone."

"Is Aileen safe?" Lazarus asked. "I will need someone to talk to and she is willing to loan me books on Innruld history and other topics to read."

He held up the book and realized he hadn't even looked at the title yet.

The spine was blank, unlike any book he had ever seen.

Even the few books that people owned in this age proudly displayed their title for the world to read when shelved.

Lazarus flipped it up and spent a moment deciphering the ornate and flowery script font that the title page presented.

*Worlds of the Masters.*

Well, that pretty much put it into perspective, didn't it?

"Yes," Wolcott responded when Lazarus looked up. "But I would suggest not letting anyone else know that you can read Innruld. She can get you more books when we arrive at Dormell, as well."

"Very good, Director," Lazarus replied, standing again. "Are there other questions I might deal with at present?"

"There are not," Wolcott said. "We should get to Dormell in five days."

Lazarus nodded and turned. The door opened and he emerged back into the hallway. Aileen Enjehn was waiting for him after all, when it had looked earlier like he wouldn't see her again today.

"News?" she asked carefully after the office hatch closed behind him.

"You're safe to know the truth, but we should not tell many details to the others," he said. "I'm a dumb spacer, so illiterate as far as everyone else is concerned. You'll have to be my big sister if they let me out on station, keeping me out of trouble."

"Okay, I can do that," she said after a moment.

Lazarus hadn't intended to trigger some maternal instincts in the tiny woman, but maybe he had. She nodded at him and smiled, heading back.

"I'm going to take a nap," she announced. "You should go read about the bastards who think they own the universe."

Lazarus watched her depart, willing to accept a dismissal when he saw one. He might have just recruited her into his own conspiracy, even if it was just to keep him from going stir crazy. Khyaa'sha was the only other crew member he'd met with whom any warmth had been evident.

But he was an alien here. And taller than most everyone else, so he stood out, and possibly reminded them of the Innruld, even if they supposedly had another foot of height on him in person. He was still a dangerous outsider, overly strong and from a radically different culture.

Still, he had time. Wolcott and Ereshkiki Nisab would hopefully decide if they were keeping him,or abandoning him on the first station they met after he got some sort of papers.

At no point had they mentioned pay. Or proper identification papers. Or anything else.

At the same time, Lazarus realized that it had been less than two days since he'd first hailed them in orbit of some unknown planet in the middle of a stellar nebula birthing new stars as fast as they could pull together enough hydrogen to generate fusion.

What insanity would a week aboard this ship bring?

# CHAPTER EIGHTEEN

## ADDISON

WHAT TO DO with the human? Addison had discussed it with Ereshkiki Nisab for some time after Lazarus had returned to his cabin to read, but they had come to no firm consensus.

He owed the human rescue and transit to a station under Innruld law. From there, the being could begin a new life. Lazarus was apparently the name for the reborn among his kind, so this would be his future, separated from the past of that battle and flight into the dangerous wilderness.

Did Addison keep Lazarus aboard as part of his crew? Certainly, that would protect most of the ship's secrets from accidental discovery later. Or intentional disclosure.

Addison looked around his personal cabin and considered how he had gotten here. He was a Director of a reasonably profitable venture, even with just the cargo he officially declared, to say nothing of those boxes that Lazarus had tucked up in a place where nobody could get them down without help.

The room betrayed its resident. All the normal sharp corners had been removed when he took out the central wall so he could have a double cabin with an elevated nest depressed in the middle. Addison kept the heat a few degrees warmer in here so he could sleep more restfully.

In his closet, a collection of shirts and vests that went with the equipment harness he habitually wore when he was off-ship. Dressing warmer than a station was rarely necessary. If it was that cold, he'd send Thadrakho out and let him deal with folks. Chances were they were Necherle anyway, if he was in that kind of climate for a delivery.

Around him, *Shiva Zephyr Glaive* was a speedy cargorunner, two points faster than the average civilian transport. The crew was a good mix of species that all got along well.

If Aileen was willing to put up with Lazarus, the human's muscles would be extremely helpful in the cargo-moving business. She had given Addison a write-up detailing an eight percent improvement in volume by being able to stack containers three and four high in odd corners without having to find a way to get the crane under the upper deck overhang.

That alone argued for keeping Lazarus aboard and being able to pay him and everyone else better.

But other parts of the human's story didn't add up. Lazarus probably wasn't even aware of the discrepancies, but partly that was a comparison of information disclosed over that first dinner with details that had come out since. Details that had *shifted* some.

Addison was nearly certain that the ship *Ajax* had not been destroyed. That Lazarus had hidden it somewhere instead. The so-called lifepod was a fully-equipped shuttle with its own trans-light drive of some sort, and not just a tiny shell you threw yourself into and then triggered the launching rockets just before your main vessel exploded.

*Warship.*

What could Addison do if he had a vessel capable of taking his war to the Innruld directly? What should he do?

There was an entire Species Underground out there that would probably vote for access to weapons capable of threatening the Innruld. *Shiva Zephyr Glaive* was armed, but that was to keep pirates at bay. Even on his best day Wybert was no threat to the massive Security Barcs that the slaves of the Innruld used to enforce the will of the overlords.

What might *Ajax* have done? Or do on some future date? Addison knew he didn't dare let Lazarus out of his sight until that question was answered.

At the same time, he would need to protect the human from his own superiors, lest one of them decided to kidnap the human in some stupid attempt to force Lazarus to show them where *Ajax* lay hidden, if the vessel did indeed still exist. Addison could see the human overwhelming his guards, especially if nobody told those people how strong the human was.

Addison felt the strangest mix of feelings come over him as he considered what lies he might suddenly decide to tell his superiors. And his enemies.

Because everyone would misunderstand the human, spy or not.

There would only be one chance to lay hands on *Ajax*. Addison could see that. Using force would just alienate the one ally that might help them change the universe.

If they played it right, Lazarus might even show them how to build copies of the vessel with which to introduce the overlords to a greater parity among the species.

Addison wondered if he would send up any red flags looking for references to the Rio Alliance when he got to Dormell. Or if he should just settle for asking one of his underworld contacts and reminding that person to keep such inquiries at a personal remove, just in case the Innruld took notice. And take exception.

The Phraettis Nebula was supposedly outside of space that the Innruld claimed, so any species beyond that were theoretically strangers, were they not? Opportunities for trade and cultural contact?

Allies one might quietly recruit?

Addison would have to allow the authorities access to Lazarus. The human would need papers, even if he only continued to crew on *Shiva Zephyr Glaive*.

But what would the authorities do or say? Would they know what humans were? And where might they have learned what a human was?

That in itself would lead Addison and his contacts to other questions. Other potential revelations.

What other species out there might the Innruld not want their underlings to meet?

# CHAPTER NINETEEN

LAZARUS

BECAUSE HE HAD BEEN a good boy, eating all his vegetables and washing behind his ears, at least metaphorically, Lazarus got to be on the bridge as *Shiva Zephyr Glaive* came out of trans-space at a place called Dormell.

One moment, that endless expanse of pearl-gray nothingness shot through with blue streaks. The next, the utter black of deep space lit with distant stars. He had never imagined what a mathematical hyperspace tunnel might look like from the inside. Back home, they were gone so fast that you left behind a huge flash of blue-shifted light as you arrived at your destination.

But he was here now. Innruld Space, shadowed behind the great shield of that nebula that had once marked the boundaries of known space as far as humans had even considered.

Kuei called up a new image on the main screen and then echoed it to the smaller one at the station where Lazarus sat next to the NavCrawler Cormac.

Fairie Castle. Lazarus couldn't think of any other term to describe what he was seeing.

Instead of a big cube, or even a torus hanging in space, someone had literally built a castle in orbit. It even had a specific bottom, a downside pointed at the surface of the blue-green planet below, flat across like an ancient stone fortress that had been torn from the earth somewhere, but this thing was metal. At least it looked like metal.

Gray mixed with all of the pastels he could imagine, like someone had taken a model they bought and swiped at it with enormous brushes to add color at random. The towers emerging from the top of the keep looked like something he had once seen on the cover of a fantasy novel he had read as a child, floating almost weightless above the ground. Those were lit up as well, while the walls of the fortress below were just rough and dark.

The ship was aligned almost perfectly on a corner as they approached, so Lazarus could see two identical gates, both open, like the ship was supposed to fly into the middle of the courtyard and land.

But that would be silly, right?

Except…

"Dormell Station Control, this is *Shiva Zephyr Glaive*," Kuei said now, her voice far more formal than normal. "Requesting docking lane and landing assignment. Details transmitted."

"Stand by, *Shiva Zephyr Glaive*," a bored, superior voice returned.

Lazarus thought it sounded like a he, but he couldn't really tell, given the octave range just within the crew.

"*Shiva Zephyr Glaive*, approach has been approved," the voice returned. "Enter via port three for customs inspection. Your information file shows an undocumented crew member. Explain."

Lazarus listened hard, but nowhere in there had he heard *please*.

"Ship-wrecked mariner, Station Control," Kuei replied smoothly. "By the time we got to him, he had nothing but the suit on his back. All cash and credentials have been lost, and we also believe he is an alien species, as we have no records of his type."

"Do we need isolation, *Shiva Zephyr Glaive*?"

"Negative, Station Control," Kuei even smiled now as he looked over at her, ears upright and tilted a little forward in her amusement. "MedCrawler records were attached as part of the original file. Appendix Seven."

She turned like she had felt his gaze upon her and smiled. It was a real smile, too. He had picked up the phrase *Sticking it to the Man* from the crew during the last few days, as an example of their opinion of Dormell Station Control. And presumably other places where the Innruld held sway.

That's where Kuei Akeley was right now.

Lazarus could imagine the dithering over there. Bureaucrats did not like randomness. It ruined their *Harmonious Approach to the All*. Didn't matter the species or the culture. And an unknown alien mariner was most certainly going to do that to somebody's day.

"Where did you pick up that creature?" the voice demanded.

"Appendix Five, Station Control," Kuei covered her mouth lest the microphone pick up the giggles emerging now.

Lazarus knew that Director Wolcott had already concocted a false trail of the last month's journeys to hide his rendezvous, so they just needed to add in a mark about a lost explorer vessel of unknown provenance, a distress signal, and then perhaps write down the coordinates wrong.

*Whoops. Not sure where we found him, then. Maybe we'll have to backtrack later. We'll let you know.*

Lazarus felt his own cheeks start to hurt with the enormous grin on his face. He glanced over at Director Wolcott and saw the same sort of glow about the man. *Naga. Churquen.*

"You are cleared to land, *Shiva Zephyr Glaive*," Station Control finally allowed grudgingly. "Expect further questions."

"Acknowledged, Station Control," Kuei managed to say and cut the line before she was overcome with the giggles.

Lazarus joined in, as did Addison Wolcott.

"Now what?" Lazarus asked when everything finally settled.

"Now we enter the dragon's maw," Wolcott said in a more serious tone. "We have to spoof the overlords and their lackeys that you are nothing worth consideration, make our next meetup, and then perhaps conduct some legitimate business. For obvious reasons, I am not about to grant you shore leave here, as we don't want to tempt anyone to do anything stupid, so you'll have to rely on Aileen and Thadrakho. Why did you recruit him, anyway?"

"He's a biped, like me," Lazarus smiled in spite of his seriousness. "Taller, too, so he can find pants that are long enough, as long as he had the circumference correct. I doubt any tailor on station would carry clothing that actually fits me without just getting it custom made. That might be a requirement, but I'm hoping Thadrakho can find something, or at least try it on if Aileen finds it. Otherwise, he's going to buy some books on pattern-making and teach himself."

"Thadrakho wants to become a tailor?" Kuei asked. "This I have to see."

"It was that, or I take all of you to my homeworld to

shop," Lazarus said. "Might yet do that, but we need to accomplish some other things first."

"Indeed, Lazarus," Wolcott acknowledged, leaving unstated, as best Lazarus could tell, all that critical subtext that had been left in the Director's office.

Lazarus knew there would come a reckoning, one of these days, but it didn't have to be today.

Or even tomorrow.

First, there was a man needed sticking to.

# CHAPTER TWENTY

ADDISON

DORMELL STATION HAD NOT CHANGED one iota since his last visit, but Addison doubted that change was ever actually allowed. The Innruld controlled everything and as long as their needs were met, up in Skycity, the port itself below would just have to make do.

He had brought Wybert along today, joining Lazarus, Aileen, and Thadrakho as they marched to the station's control node inside a ring of a half-dozen security troopers of various species.

Wybert was armed, but everyone understood that taking a powerspear away from an Ilount required a greater reason than this. Everyone else had left weapons back on the ship, though.

There wasn't much the group of them could do if the overlords were feeling pissy, except to submit to their authority and file whatever legal grievances were necessary for Addison to alert his own superiors somewhere that they had an agent in trouble.

And given the situation, those worthies might not react, since they currently had no idea of the value of the tall human in their midst. And Addison dare say nothing if he was in custody, as the servants of the *Great Ones* would be listening in, legal or not.

Addison found it amusing watching Lazarus walk. Thadrakho's legs were only a little longer, for all his extra height, but Necherle moved with graceful deliberation they learned on the ice and snow of home at a young age, so Thadrakho's normal speed was comparable to Aileen's. Wybert clattered along in a noisy mass of sound, while Addison set the pace as he slithered along.

Lazarus was used to walking much faster. And it wasn't just those long legs, although that helped. The gravity was even lower on station than the ship, but Addison kept his ship a few points high for the extra exercise of lifting yourself when you weighed more.

Lazarus must feel like he was on the verge of flying at times.

Interestingly, news of the human must have leaked, as Addison found a larger than normal number of onlookers, standing suspiciously around as his group trooped through the cold, steel corridors of the port. There were many species taller than a human. Necherle for example, to say nothing of the Innruld themselves, but Addison had never met anyone with the mass density of a human. And Lazarus claimed to be of average height and weight for a male of his species.

Addison didn't want to think about the largest examples of humans that Lazarus had described. What species was supposed to have that great a range of normal distributions? What evolutionary pressures generated *that*?

But the guards kept everyone at a safe distance, observing and tittering behind raised hands for the most part. Lazarus was a kit in a candy store, head rotating every which way as he saw many more species of citizen than he had probably imagined, especially if the Rio Alliance represented a total of only four.

Addison could see more than thirty, just on this long concourse.

Finally, they came to the hatch Addison had been dreading. He had made eye contact with a few folks as he slithered along, passing subtle signals with hands and eye ridges that he had important information for folks.

As if landing at Dormell with a representative of an unknown species might have been just a minor thing.

They were met at the portal by an Innruld representative of Skycity itself, which immediately threw out about half of Addison's plans. He had hoped that the masters paid no attention to the alien, but apparently someone had decided to inquire.

The lord was male. A little over seven feet tall, but weighed probably the same as Lazarus. Addison suddenly realized what a threat a human might represent, seeing his bulk next to the ethereal nature of the Innruld. No species had the pure beauty of the Innruld. Legend had it that they had once bred and engineered themselves to be the most beautiful creatures in space.

Addison could see a measure of truth to that. This one had the long, lean face the Innruld prized. Large green eyes and a tapering jaw that came nearly to a point.

Even for a Churquen, Addison could see how much heavier and brutish Lazarus looked. Unevolved, perhaps. Certainly ugly by Innruld standards, even as the two species were probably the closest in physical form.

Addison managed to suppress the giggle that wanted to escape as he considered that Thadrakho and Aileen might end up having to dress Lazarus as an Innruld, just because nobody else's clothes would be as good a fit.

Lazarus, Director and Overlord.

Oh, what a wonderful practical joke that would be to play.

Maybe if he could convince the human to share the secrets of *Ajax* with them, they would dress the human as an Innruld Command Leader.

After all, Addison could only be executed for treason once.

"The rest of you will wait out here," the Innruld officer announced.

"I am responsible for the human," Addison pushed back subtly. "He is without papers or identity, and has only a limited grasp of the language. Plus, his accent is atrocious."

"Do you understand me?" the Innruld demanded of Lazarus, body language a little chilled from what Addison could see. Height and weight made Lazarus a physical threat in ways no other species but a Qooph with a running start represented.

"Some," Lazarus replied harshly. "Are authority?"

Again, Addison had steeled himself not to laugh out loud at the games Lazarus was prepared to play. The human had read three books on Innruld history and culture on the way in, and the human was pretending to be little more than a trained Wahqf.

"Fine," the Innruld sighed in an exaggerated and exasperated manner. "You will join us and translate, Director Wolcott."

Addison nodded to the overlord and then to the rest of his crew. They had gamed this out, so everyone had assignments and this had been the most likely scenario going in.

Now he had to convince the masters to ignore a simple human, without ever realizing that Lazarus might proclaim their doom.

If Addison played his cards right.

# CHAPTER TWENTY-ONE

## LAZARUS

HOW TO PLAY a bumbling fool that had no clue about much of anything and only a limited grasp of the language? Lazarus understood the need. And Wolcott had promised him greater freedom at the next station stop, once the excitement of a newly-discovered species died down.

Assuming it did.

Lazarus had spoken a few more times with Wolcott in his office. The Churquen potentially represented the same sort of rebellion against Innruld authority that the Rio Alliance did Westphalia, if Lazarus understood the subtext of certain comments correctly.

But they had to cut the Gordian Knot here first, and a blade was not necessarily an option. At least not today.

"Sit there," the Innruld security bureaucrat gestured at a chair meant for someone taller.

Lazarus would look like a child, with his feet swinging, but he supposed that the purpose here was to reinforce the authority of the tallest species. Even Necherle weren't quite up to the height standards of the Innruld.

But Lazarus did as he was told. And it would help him

remain in character as perhaps a semi-precocious ten-year-old.

He could always stumble over words or ask Wolcott to repeat something, if he wanted to manipulate the emotions of the room.

The agent of the overlords sat behind a large desk in a chair fitted to him. The desk was also closer to something Lazarus would have stood at, rather than sitting behind.

Three of the guards had accompanied him into the large office, and stood along the wall behind the chair where Lazarus sat, with Wolcott coiled up beside him as if all this was perfectly normal.

Lazarus didn't recognize the species of the nearest guard, but he had a couple of guesses he could make. Biped like him, but roughly five feet tall and slender in Lazarus's eyes, although probably much stronger and heavier than most of the rest.

Having shoulders on a solid torso allowed a much greater upper body strength, and apparently the human level of musculature was rare or unknown here.

"Name?" the officer asked bluntly, a finger pointed at Lazarus.

The hand had three impossibly-long fingers and a thumb, reminding Lazarus of a hairless orangutan in a way.

"Lazarus," he replied. Just for fun, he slowly spelled it in Interlac, and then sounded the word out slowly on the assumption that someone was recording all this and would use that to make him papers later.

Assuming he made it out of this office alive and free. Addison Wolcott had placed such odds as low, but not impossible.

"Species?"

"Human."

"Planet of origin?"

Lazarus looked confused. Leaned his head forward and ruffled his brow together. The lips pursed. He turned to Wolcott.

"Homeworld, Lazarus?" the Director asked.

"Ah," Lazarus relaxed and smiled. "Brasilia."

"Coordinates?"

Lazarus just tilted his head slightly and blinked. He could even be honest here, mostly because he had made a point to not try to calculate the path home yet. He had no way to get there at the moment, and the distance would shock most of the people he might tell.

Addison Wolcott probably wouldn't even blink, but he ran far deeper than he looked. Maybe deeper than Lazarus.

Lazarus shrugged. It was apparently a universal thing in species with shoulders. The bureaucrat grumbled.

"How can this thing not know his coordinates?" he demanded, turning his attention to Wolcott now as Lazarus watched.

"I presume he was not born on an Innruld world, Your Grace," Wolcott's tone got oily and supercilious in a way that conveyed the utter irrelevance of all other planets.

Lazarus maintained a wide-eyed innocence as he wondered who was on first, according to the ancient, ritual joke.

"Is this true?" The officer's eyes came back this way.

Lazarus assumed the emotion he was seeing split the difference between outrage and confusion. Didn't every child learn their coordinates not long after they learned their home address?

"Sir?" Lazarus couldn't help himself.

"Where is this…Brasilia?" the officer demanded.

Lazarus let his face get big and wide and confused and sorry and whatever else he could get away with. The big, elaborate pantomime of a shrug with hands moving outwards was probably a little too much icing on the cake, but Lazarus was seeing a species that considered itself so superior to everyone else in the galaxy that he couldn't have stopped himself if he wanted.

Sticking it to the man.

Lazarus could see a tall, stunningly-beautiful species using that beauty to intimidate the morlocks of the galaxy, like Lazarus. He would be good and not do anything about it.

Today.

"Has he any skills or training credentials?" The officer pivoted back to Wolcott like a ping-pong ball.

"He takes direction well, and has been assisting my Loadmaster with his strength," Wolcott said. "As you note, he speaks some Innruld, but we're not sure where he learned it, and seems to have suffered some trauma in the process."

"There was another ship you served on?" the officer demanded, almost rising out of his chair at the apparent thought of someone not filling out the correct forms. "Whose?"

Bureaucrats didn't know a higher crime, anywhere in the galaxy.

Lazarus shuddered in supposed fear and turned in on himself, body language collapsing into a defensive, protective shell.

*Just another helpless victim, your honor.*

As planned, he turned to Wolcott and blinked several times, working up a good hyperventilation act as he did.

"It's okay, Lazarus," Wolcott soothed. "You can tell them."

Lazarus had no idea who Wolcott and Kuei were setting up, but the rest of the crew had a similarly low opinion, when the topic came up, even if names were never mentioned.

"Akeley," Lazarus murmured in a hard slur. "Lots of them."

"What's he saying?" the officer roared.

"I believe, from the bits he has been willing to share through his fear, that Lazarus previously served in some capacity aboard a cargo vessel with a crew of only Vaadwig," Wolcott turned Shakespearean on them all. "He reacted with panic the first time he met my Helmsman, Kuei Akeley, fearing her. Only after we convinced him otherwise has he relaxed enough to be useful."

"Vaadwig, huh?" the officer's voice got ugly.

It was the sort of thing that promised forensic audits going back decades.

Bureaucrats thwarted. Never a pleasant experience.

Lazarus noted the glance that passed between the officer and one of the goons standing behind him. It was a look of knowing. Perhaps suspicions were being accidentally confirmed?

Someone else getting theirs?

He felt a little bad to be doing something like that to a total stranger, but Lazarus needed this ship, this crew. They had proven friendly, after the rough start for which Wybert tended to apologize for at least daily.

"So we suspect, Your Grace," Wolcott simpered. "We might not ever know the truth."

But from the look in the being's eyes, Lazarus suspected that whatever ship was being set up right now would have a masterfully-rough, ugly time on their next station call.

He wondered if messages would be sent to other stations to lock that ship down, whoever they were, until someone could dissect their records sufficiently to prove that they weren't the ones withholding evidence of a new species.

Proving the dog didn't bark was perhaps the hardest task of all.

"So what will you do with the creature?" the Innruld asked Wolcott now, as if Lazarus wasn't present, or linguistically capable.

"Innruld law required that we rescue him and transport him as far as our next station stop, Your Grace," Wolcott's voice got fearful and almost timid, which Lazarus found amusing. "From there, I need to get him papers so he exists in your systems, and determine what he would like to do next. I would hire him on with my crew, partly out of sentiment and partly because he has been a good worker. But he is presumably a free being."

Lazarus liked the implication that perhaps freedom wasn't necessarily a widespread thing in Innruld space. Wolcott didn't suggest that the overlords weren't a just and caring superior class. One did not do that with their kind, not if one wished to survive, but you could skate that fine edge, especially if you have just rescued someone from death and are helping those same authorities track down the blackguards that may have not filled out all the necessary forms in triplicate.

"And to discover the secret of his origins?" the bureaucrat got a new light in his eyes. Just as cunning but not as violent. "Open a new trade route?"

"Presumably there is at least one planet of his kind unserved by Innruld trade, my lord," Wolcott caught the tone and seemingly joined the creature in a conspiracy of mercantilism. "I see no reason that a Vaadwig ship should garner all those profits. Perhaps I will need to undertake a few voyages of discovery. One hopes that the planet lies somewhere near to Dormell, so we can continue to use this Station as a trade base from which we might all grow wealthy."

Lazarus liked the gleam of pure avarice that appeared in

the bureaucrat's eyes for a moment. An untapped planetary market? Merchants needing to haul goods from Dormell?

Who wouldn't want to get rich in the next gold rush?

They just needed the idiot human to finally remember what part of the sky he came from.

It made a lovely game. Wolcott was apparently the master of it, well in advance of this Innruld bureaucrat for whom it was probably just a task that couldn't necessarily be foisted off on one of the lesser species. Especially not if they could get rich.

*Can't have the lesser species growing powerful now, can we?*

Lazarus hoped he could somehow engineer a meeting of the Innruld with Westphalia. Let the human supremacists run headlong into the overlords of the galaxy and fight it out. The Rio Alliance could use allies, but not the Innruld. Churquen. Qooph. Yithadreph. Even Vaadwig, as long as the rest eventually forgave him for the nasty practical joke he was about to play on one of their captains.

Still, they appeared to be over the hump. The Innruld opened a drawer on his side of the desk and pulled out the ultimate weapon of the modern bureaucrat: the clipboard with its triplicate form.

"Fill in as much as you know," the being ordered Wolcott, assuming without any evidence at all that Lazarus was illiterate in Interlac/Innruld. "We will have him update the records as we learn more or he grows more linguistically adept."

"As you command, Your Grace," Wolcott replied, taking the weapon and pulling out a pen with which to do battle.

Lazarus watched, innocent as a doe. Wolcott never looked up, nor asked any questions, just filled things in while leaving most of it blank.

They had Lazarus sign the bottom with a scrawl his own mother would not have recognized, and then it was back onto that long concourse of the station port. Pictures had been submitted already, so at some point Lazarus would hopefully be issued a standard Innruld identity card. Under an assumed name. As a lost refugee from unknown space.

Maybe planning a revolution.

# CHAPTER TWENTY-TWO

AILEEN

SHE DIDN'T LIKE PEOPLE. Noise. Chaos. Overload.

That was why Aileen liked cargo. Simple problems. Simple solutions. Cure the ship's emptiness with the fewest number of moves now or tomorrow.

The rest of the crew understood that about her. Left her alone most of the time. Let her assemble and disassemble her cargo bays her way, just putting their muscle to work when she needed to change the configuration on an evolving basis.

She'd been dead nervous about Lazarus. That size screamed predator to her subconscious. Male didn't help, especially coupled with bulk.

The shower had been a trap, to see how the human would react to her nudity. Her perceived vulnerability. With Wybert and Remahle armed and hiding close by, in case they needed to get involved and zap him with something.

Nobody had mentioned anything to Addison. Wasn't any need. Lazarus had mopped the deck without complaint. Scrubbed her back without comment, even though she knew from the look in his eyes that the female human form must look substantially like her, presumably without the whiskers and fur, but similar shape.

And they had breasts. He had stared at hers more than once, but never stayed even within arm's length longer than necessary. Never let his hands wander to where his eyes might have strayed. Behaved himself around total strangers.

The human was an officer. Had been one in command of his own ship before this, from his stories. But he also took orders without complaint. Listened to Kuei, Khyaa'sha, and the Loadmaster without any of that male guff. Took orders, executed, waited for more.

Asked to borrow a book politely, read it, and returned it with a speed that told her how literate he really was, moving on to the next book.

Addison had him back on the ship now, buttoned up against any of the locals deciding to capture him for a circus or something. She was in charge of Thadrakho and a shopping list, at least until the Innruld dipshit in charge got over himself and lifted the cargo isolation on them that he had slapped around an unknown species.

Nothing in the bays was time-critical. Addison had already built slack into the schedule because he had needed to go somewhere without the Innruld being any the wiser.

They'd be cleared by tomorrow, if the locals held to form, and she could get rid of two of those six boxes along with about a third of the rest. Then move on and get loaded for the run to Aceanx and the next two boxes.

She'd be glad when the stuff was gone. She wasn't a rebel in any hard sense of the word, but didn't like the Innruld any more than the rest of the crew. Those boxes would destroy lives when the contents made their way into those oh-so-delicate salons in the Skycity above her, or the others around the universe.

Maybe break the Innruld. Or just give them something

else to do instead of breeding the next generation, and they could kill themselves off and make the galaxy a better place.

But that was tomorrow's problem. Today, she had Thadrakho and shopping needs for Lazarus. And she needed to do it, because nobody else really read books and Addison had given her some extra cash to start a ship's library. More than what they already had electronically, but Aileen liked the feel of waterproof pages under her fingers.

Thadrakho followed quietly, like he did. The man lived for instructions from his nest queens, so he just automatically defaulted to subordinate around her, especially since she was usually moving boxes around and his height was helpful, even if Lazarus was so much stronger.

Nobody was following them, as near as she could tell. Not that what she was doing was any great secret, but she felt better being anonymous. Addison had modified her marching orders slightly, so she found herself in a shop that largely specialized in Innruld fashion. Per her cohorts, anything big enough around the waist and thighs was fine, as the legs could be cut off later to the right height.

She felt like a child walking into the store. Thadrakho behind her didn't help, as he was almost as tall as the manikins in here.

How could anyone control legs that long? Or keep arms from hitting everything when you moved? Must work, both the humans and the Innruld had arrived at the same design independently.

"What need brings you?" the merchant asked, looking forever down than long, elegant nose at her and sneering that way he probably did with any of the *lesser species*.

A Yithadreph shopkeeper would have asked *"How can I help you today, mistress?"* and been smiling.

Aileen swallowed the retort on her tongue and flexed her whiskers forward solicitously.

"Alien crew member needs new clothing, but is confined to ship," she answered flatly. "Erect biped. Six feet tall. Heavier than the Innruld, but of the same basic design outline. Pants, shirts, outerwear. Shoes will be custom-made later."

"The human," he said without emotion.

"The human," Aileen agreed. "My Director felt that Innruld might be a good fit for start, if we can find something wide enough."

She could see avarice at being the man who dressed the human warring with species distaste in his eyes. What would it do to his reputation to be known for also dressing humans? Would he be able to carry another line of clothing as a new species came to station?

She looked around while the man stewed. Shirts and vests were generally available anywhere, as most species had shoulders and arms where you could always cut off or roll up sleeves, depending, if you could find the tremendous circumference humans had.

Pants were where they differentiated themselves.

"What are the human's measurements?" the merchant finally asked, his greed apparently greater than his superiority.

Aileen pulled out the piece of paper Lazarus had translated and read them off.

"Color?"

"He's been in red from his emergency kit since we rescued him," she felt like sticking a knife into the conversation, just because. "I'm more interested in size and fit. Color can come later."

"He wore a Clan design on his back earlier," the man said. "Do we know the parentage?"

Trust a tailor to notice that first. And assume it was his coat of arms.

Aileen decided to be a little extra mean. The shopkeeper was another one of those oh-so-superior Innruld.

"I could get a picture of the design, if you think it might be reproducible," she said, laughing inside at the thought of Innruld overlords advertising for a human brewery, however innocently.

Lazarus had found it amusing that he did. What might the rest of Innruld space be like if she could pull a fast one?

"Do we know which Heraldic Officer of their College of Arms should be consulted?" he asked, suddenly breathless that he might be dealing with rich nobility instead of a poor spacer.

"We have not yet identified his homeworld," Aileen snapped. "I will consult with him and see what his laws and heritage allow."

Like, advertising a human drinks manufacturer, for a liquid most species consider poisonous, in a place no human has ever heard of.

*Screw you, buddy.*

But she never let that thought anywhere near her whiskers. Too much risk he might be able to read her if she did. And the best revenge on the overlords that she could think of was to make them look silly.

"This way." The shopkeeper led her deep into the store, towards a section in the back she wanted to translate as *Fat Innruld Clothing*. Certainly the cuts were generous, compared to the pale leanness of the masters. Lazarus was a foot shorter and probably comparable in weight to most Innruld, but she had never seen a fat one before.

Didn't know they came that big around. Better, some of them must be short and rotund, because she found several set of pants that would almost fit as is.

Shirts were impossible here, as she looked around. Even the spherical Innruld didn't have the shoulders of a human.

She wondered if anyone did, or if they would need to just find something stretchy enough to wear like a second skin to keep him warm.

*Now you see why I have fur.*

Bottom half done, she took Thadrakho to a pawn shop that specialized in *weird*. Space was always a bizarre place to work, but most of your equipment was fairly standard. There were only so many ways to interpret physics.

Thadrakho, however, had been in here before. He took her to the back and she swore the Necherle was drooling as he ran his hands over a piece of equipment she couldn't have identified if her life depended on it.

"Okay, I give," Aileen said. "What is it?"

"Sewing machine," he clicked back at her, all four antennae stuck straight out in excitement. "I can learn human patterns and adjust things. Or make them from bolts of cloth."

Necherle were weird. No two ways about it. But service to the nest was baked into his genetic structure, and he had accepted Lazarus as one of them.

And didn't the galaxy need more Necherle tailors?

Aileen looked at the price and blanched.

"That's how much a used one costs?" she asked Thadrakho, shocked.

"Industrial model," his voice oozed excitement through the clicks. "And I can afford."

Huh. Addison certainly hadn't given her nearly enough funds for something like that anyway. But if Thadrakho was all in on buying it for himself, she could stretch funds for fabric and supplies.

What would a human look good wearing, without any fur but the reddish-blond on top?

While Thadrakho and the shopkeeper Vaadwig dickered over price, Aileen wandered the rest of the store. It wasn't one she was familiar with, but obviously her shipmate had been in here before, as he walked right to the machine he wanted.

There were books. She touched them lovingly. Addison mostly kept entertainment stuff for the readers, but she preferred histories and biographies over escapism. Plus, she had a human to educate.

Two books seemed adequately interesting. She grabbed a third one, kind of a high school primer on Innruld Space that was truthful enough for someone just starting out. Fabric wasn't something this store did, but she knew others on the station, closer to the Skycity elevators, where choices would improve.

Aileen watched Thadrakho pushing the wheeled cart that held his new toy up to the counter and pull a wad of bills from his bandolier, humming to himself with excitement. They paid for everything and headed back to the ship with this first load, and to let others have a station break before her next expedition.

And maybe, just maybe she could convince Lazarus to let her take a really good picture of that beer company logo.

# CHAPTER TWENTY-THREE

## ADDISON

DORMELL WASN'T A QUIVERING mass of rebellion just awaiting a spark, but there were still angry people to be found, if you knew where to look. Addison had left Ereshkiki Nisab in charge of the ship and wandered down into some of the darker places on the docks, where the beautiful people never went, and might not even send their armed servants in small groups.

It wasn't unsafe, for civilians. Only intruders who might be spies, or gendarmes thinking the citizens they encountered here were law abiding and friendly.

Addison knocked on a particular hatch that wasn't ever left open during business hours. An eyehole slid open and three eyes peered out at him.

So, the Kreeghal, Vallas, was on duty today. Good to know.

Those three eyes studied him closely for a moment, unblinking and dark green, then looked around behind him before the woman grunted to herself and closed the eyehole. The hatch itself slid into the wall a moment later and Vallas almost smiled at him as he entered.

Kreeghal were the next step squished for the bipeds, even smaller than a human. Four and a half feet tall, male or female, give or take. Innruld weight on legs not much longer than Aileen's. Longer arms, so maybe a Kreeghal shirt would fit Lazarus's shoulders, but the human's torso was far too long, unless they found some sort of dress tunic that normally came down to Vallas's knees.

She turned her attention back to the corridor behind Addison until he was past the hatch and then triggered the mechanism to close it again and seal him in.

The room was surprisingly well-lit for a dark back room where illegal deals were frequently made. Wooden tables and a few benches of a higher quality than this area of the docks should have had.

Addison looked at the bar and snickered to himself. Lazarus had explained the immense range of ethyl alcohols humans regularly consumed: by color, taste, base ingredients, and apparent toxicity. But humans also had the concept of a tea room, so Lazarus would have probably fit in just fine here.

Addison made his way to an empty table well away from the half-dozen others in here and coiled himself. The Tea House Keeper was an ancient Mizanet who moved with the deliberation of his age, oozing slowly across the floor on a monopod like the giant land snail he was.

Addison wondered if the man moved at the pace just so the tea was properly steeped when it arrived, or if that was just luck. Tea took a while, but Addison wasn't in a hurry.

Ameqran the Mizanet was built roughly like Wybert the Ilount, except his vertical parts were in the center of a single long foot, rather than at the front of the ten-footed-body. He had the four arms like Wybert on his torso, but moved on a single, enormous foot that could slither across broken glass or burning coals for as long as the man could hold his breath.

The tea was perfect when it arrived. Ameqran was like that. Addison paid and nodded as the man slowly retreated to his bar, a polite glacier that made quiet, squishy sounds as he crossed the metal deck, even if he left no trail.

Addison sipped at the tea, but he already knew it would be too hot, so he leaned back on his coil and studied the room. Mostly Directors of one sort or another, plus the merchants that they dealt directly with. Because this was a closed society, admission by invitation only. Innruld and their friends need not apply.

His contact emerged from a rear chamber and Addison felt his breath speed up, just the slightest bit. Churquen were rare in this sector of space, but a woman like Eha would have stood out in a room filled with their kind, long graceful stripes starting at her neck and running almost to the tip of her tail, dark amber honey painted on an emerald background.

Addison remembered to keep his jaw from falling open and cursed the cover identities that kept him from courting this woman openly. They had more important duties to the nest than mating, although he would have gladly given up his spy games for her.

Eha, however, was all business, all the time. Honey colored eyes focused on him as she slithered close and they briefly entwined in greeting before she coiled nearby. Not across the round table, but on his left, just out of immediate reach.

She had brought her own tea in a mug, unnoticed as he had seen nothing but her beauty crossing the floor. Hopefully there weren't any police waiting to storm the building, as she might blind him completely and he'd end up in a cell.

Except Addison knew that a cell would only be temporary, once they figured out what he was really up to.

"Station gossip suggests you had an adventure on your most recent run," Eha opined obliquely.

"It's even more complicated than that," Addison replied in a quiet, gruff tone. "We're dealing with what appears to be a previously-unknown, technological species from outside Innruld Space."

"Is it dangerous?" She leaned forward a little and sipped daintily.

"That remains to be seen," he replied, joining her. "I have hopes that we can befriend him well enough that he will lead us to more of his kind and help us recruit."

"So you think we should leave him in your care?" Eha asked, aiming those pretty eyes at him like a ship's cannon.

"For now," Addison temporized. "My crew has welcomed him and he seems to be relaxing, but the human holds many secrets that might be lost if he decided he wasn't among allies and friends."

Addison hoped that would be sufficient to deter her. She had the authority to order him to turn the human over to her custody, if she chose to exercise it, but Eha rarely overruled him.

She studied him now in ways that made him feel slightly uncomfortable. Like she knew his secrets and was considering revealing them.

"And your other cargo?" she finally asked, bemused, if anything.

"Dormell shortly, then Aceanx, and Zhoonarrim," he replied, listing his next three stops. "That part proceeds according to schedule."

Two boxes at each, termites quietly nibbling slowly away at the foundations of Innruld power, until it fell in on itself in a future storm.

"Does the human raise your profile unacceptably?" Eha

asked, getting right to the heart of Addison's personal qualms over the last week.

*Ajax* was out there somewhere. It was a matter of convincing Lazarus to help them in the coming war as more than just another Kreeghal bouncer, like Vallas guarding the doorway. And perhaps sending aid to the Rio Alliance in their own war against Westphalia's human supremacists.

Or aiming the Innruld at Westphalia and letting the titans grind each other down with their supposed genetic superiority over all other species. But he didn't dare tell Eha that. Not today.

Even those secrets could not be held long enough to protect the key players.

"It might," Addison admitted. "The Innruld and others will certainly want to know more about human capability and coordinates, if only for the trade potentials I myself wish to exploit. I have wondered this last week if I should complete this run, but not take on any others, while I try to figure out the best way to exploit this new development."

"Can the humans help?"

"It is my fervent belief that Lazarus might be able to tip the scales significantly," Addison replied, focusing his eyes on the woman. "But that he might not be safe, even in your hands, because someone might come to understand the threat his mere existence presents and assassinate him to preserve other secrets."

"How did the Innruld react to the human?" she changed topic smoothly.

"Lazarus and I had prepared an improvisational comedic routine," Addison felt himself finally smile. "Dumb sailor, barely able to speak common. Exasperated Director just trying to follow all of the Innruld's laws and ethical standards to get the human someplace safe. Nobody knows the coordinates of his homeworld, but Lazarus has mentioned to me two stellar nations in his sector of the galaxy, one of which might be a potential ally."

"And this other?" Eha asked.

"According to the human, they would likely seek armed conflict with the Innruld," Addison replied. "Enemy of my enemy who should both be encouraged to fight amongst themselves."

"You've certainly landed in the pond," she laughed lightly. "Try not to drown?"

Addison shivered in spite of himself. His kind did not swim well. A few cousin species preferred the water, but Churquen were land dwellers.

"As long as the waters are calm, there is hope," Addison quoted the rest of the saying back to her. "Patience and care will see me to shore."

"And after Zhoonarrim?" Eha asked. "Turn you and *Shiva Zephyr Glaive* into free agents for a time?"

"There is a strong likelihood, if the waters remain placid, that Lazarus will allow us to visit his homeworld, Eha," Addison turned deadly serious. "That human can lift a hundred-pound shipping box over his head in my cargo bay and stack them three and maybe four tall, depending on the ceilings. What would a mob of such creatures do? Vallas and her kind could hold their own, but how many other species could say the same?"

"Is it safe for us?" she asked, suddenly a little breathless.

"I think so," Addison said. "Lazarus claims to be part of a political entity made up of humans, Moah, Gnashiiley, and Atomarsk."

"Atomarsk?" she gasped. "Is that possible?"

"He described them accurately, according to the oldest records, Eha," Addison stated. "Before he knew that they had faded to legend in Innruld Space."

"Then that would suggest his homeworld was located—"

Addison cut her off with a hand before she completed the thought.

"It is critical that nobody knows that information, Eha," he leaned forward and whispered sharply. "That you not tell your superiors, lest they decide to go looking in what you and I suspect might be close enough to the right direction."

"The human's enemies?" she whispered back.

"Not just that," Addison agreed. "Lazarus has secrets, even from his own kind. If we can convince him to help us then those secrets, that power, might be ours."

"If I tell my own leaders, they will advocate for taking custody of the human, Addison," Eha pointed out.

"And that is why I ask you to deflect them for now," he replied. "Buy me time to find out what the human will share. We will only have one opportunity at him. If we spoil it in our haste, we will gain nothing and lose so much possibility."

"You know things," she accused.

"I suspect things," he tempered. "I cannot know without Lazarus telling me. Showing me. He will not, if he feels we are potentially no better than the Innruld."

"You demand much, Addison Wolcott," Eha stated, but she also leaned back onto her coil and studied him. There was the hint of a smile in those golden eyes.

He watched this beautiful woman weigh his fate.

"Until Zhoonarrim, you are obligated with a previous mission," she finally said. "After that, somebody will be in touch."

She rose, tea in hand, and departed, slithering gracefully across the room and through an interior door into the depths of the building. Addison had never been back there to know what he might find, other than perhaps the heart of a conspiracy.

Or nothing at all. His cell leader issued orders and

missions. He took them. Executed them while trying to also make an honest enough profit that he could continue working Innruld Space.

But what might await him, await them all, after Zhoonarrim?

# CHAPTER TWENTY-FOUR

LAZARUS

ACEANX. Yet another Innruld world Lazarus had never heard of just a month ago.

He felt like a spacer finally though, as the station locks engaged and the platform the ship had landed on was pulled into a sealed chamber on a big slider, so air could flood in around them.

Aileen had found all manner of cloth bolts for him at Dormell, and Thadrakho had taught himself how to make clothing in a variety of styles. Lazarus had spent too much time in an organized military previously to appreciate the expense and effort associated with new clothing, and the impetus to make it whenever possible instead.

Clothing was something you just requisitioned when you wore it out.

But Addison's crew had to take care of themselves. It wasn't even like *Ajax*, where there was an entire store room dedicated to spare uniforms in all the sizes his crew had represented.

Worse, nobody was shaped like a human, anywhere he had researched. Arms and shoulders reminded him of a T-

Rex on many species, spindly enough to manipulate tools, but not to throw spears or carry heavy stones or swords into battle.

But he had clothing now, enough to do laundry without being naked at the time. Durable pants that even fit reasonably well, although Aileen had grinned at him when she presented the bolts of cloth she had found. Apparently, the exact same shade of crimson had been available, so now he had two pair in black and two more nearly identical to the original pants.

He had also made the mistake of suggesting a kilt to Thadrakho when the Necherle asked. Thadrakho had even managed to adapt something else into a pleated and paneled warrior skirt Lazarus could wear when he was feeling feisty.

Not today, but soon.

Shirts had gone one of two ways. Either skin-tight and stretched over him, or loose all over, with wrinkly shoulder seams.

Again, Lazarus had never considered how clothing was made, just that it was. He had developed a much greater appreciation for the people who could sew shoulder seams like this, as well as Thadrakho's exquisite patience. The first attempt had been an utter failure, but the man had undone it, resewn it two more times, and taught himself how to attach a sleeve. That was apparently an advanced skill comparable to plotting navigational courses through deep space.

Shoes would be a necessary mission in another six months or so, but Lazarus could wait. He had money burning a hole in his pocket and Addison had allowed him station leave shortly, supervised by both Aileen and Wybert. Adventures, but first they had to deal with the cargo unloading.

Aileen smiled up at him now, as if she could read his

mind. As his mother liked to say, men weren't much more complicated than mud puddles, and Lazarus couldn't really argue that today.

Keep *Ajax* hidden. Keep himself safe in an alien culture until he could return to her and get home. Learn as much as he could about these people until then.

Today, however, he was assisting with cargo unloading. Remahle was in charge of driving the lifter sled they had broken out again, perched on a stool and maneuvering it just so. Remahle and Aileen normally had the effort to unload things, sometimes with Kuei's help if something was heavy, but Lazarus had been slotted in as Aileen's assistant now.

And Aceanx wasn't nearly as priggish about bureaucracy, so they could unload fairly quickly. That, or the message of an alien species had already arrived ahead of them, and all the excitement had died down.

Lazarus was still just getting used to being the tallest person around, anytime that Thadrakho was over in the Machine Room fixing things. He'd been about in the middle among the men on *Ajax*, and taller than most of the women.

Here, most folks were at least half a head shorter than him, excepting only the Innruld he might meet. As a *dirty alien*, Lazarus doubted any would come looking, unless they brought a lot of trouble with them.

Addison had explained to him that the crew would do everything they could to protect their newest mate, but that there were limits, unless the Innruld forced them to turn completely outlaw.

Lazarus hoped that it would be unnecessary. There were too many potential allies the Rio Alliance could recruit here, if they did it quietly enough that the Innruld missed ships and crews wandering off.

"Ready to be a show Galumph?" Aileen asked with a

twist to her whiskers and a grin that went all the way up to her ears.

Lazarus rolled his eyes at the Yithadreph woman and sighed theatrically. Aileen and Remahle both laughed.

It felt good, belonging. Weird, but good.

The dock hissed around them loudly enough that they could hear it through the cargo hatch. After a few minutes, a hammer banged loudly on the hull, indicating that the customs inspectors had arrived outside the ship.

Aileen reached out and triggered the elevator lift to lower them to the deck outside. The rear lift connected forward to the main cargo bay and sideways to the spare bay, with Wybert's truck stored opposite the secondary bay, on the portmost part of the curve, behind the engines.

Because they were on a station, they didn't need the 10-wheel flatbed tracked crawler with crane and aft winch that was configured for Wybert to drive. That was for times when *Shiva Zephyr Glaive* had to land on a planet that didn't necessarily have first-rate port facilities.

Lazarus wondered which job Wybert would pick, gunner or driver, if Addison added some sort of a weapon's turret to the truck for hostile engagements. He didn't suggest it to anyone, though.

Today, they had the simple lifter. Aileen stood to port, and Lazarus was on the starboard side, as they descended, landing on the deck with a thump.

Sure enough, an Innruld customs officer with a lot of braid on his collar and turquoise jacket had come, along with a couple of low-ranking guards in blue, representing species that Lazarus didn't know on sight, although the short, squat one with three eyes was probably a Kreeghal, from the descriptions.

He had his passport in a pocket inside his jacket, less than half filled in with critical information, but he also knew he was the exotic on this run. Everyone would want to see.

He shrugged internally as the Innruld stepped onto the platform and towered over everyone. He looked like he enjoyed doing that to people. Lazarus had met his kind in bars a time or two.

*All that height was nice, but your knees are right up where I can get to them, if I want to get mean.*

"Papers," the man demanded of all of them.

Lazarus smiled and presented his. Aileen and Remahle got a perfunctory inspection, but they'd been on this station before. Lazarus stood perfectly still with a slightly-vacuous smile as the officer compared his face to the picture.

Innruld had bluish-gold eyes with no whites. Hauntingly beautiful, in that quiet, cold manner of a lump of radioactive cobalt. They stared at him now with about the same warmth.

Growing a beard would really mess with these folks, as most species either already had fur on their faces, like Yithadreph, or didn't possess whiskers, like the Innruld. But Addison had made him promise to behave, at least on the first run through these places. Thadrakho had made him something like a straight-razor to shave with.

Later, he might push a few boundaries, once he was no longer so strange.

"Cargo?" the officer finally handed back Lazarus's gray passport, which got tucked away.

"Here," Aileen replied in a tight tone that didn't *quite* mimic the officer's as she handed him the holiest of holies, a clipboard with paperwork.

The officer took it and began tracking box numbers against crates.

The sled was six feet wide and about ten long, with the last two of that being Remahle's stool to drive and see. Under Aileen's expert eye, Lazarus had covered over the entire surface with a jigsaw puzzle of crates, and then a second row over that.

"You will need to unload this sled," the officer snapped peevishly.

"Understood," Aileen smiled lethargically. "Lazarus, box 22753 first."

Lazarus took a second to identify the one she wanted, closest to him on the front corner. Like maybe she planned it that way. He lifted it with a grunt and waddled to the side of the lift platform to set it down.

As he turned back, the two guards and the customs officer were standing there with jaws open in raw shock. Must be a universal thing. Made them all look almost comically human.

Lazarus looked at them blankly and grabbed the next crate aftwards from the first. It went perfectly aligned with 22753 on the lift deck so that he had the arrangement still set when Aileen wanted them put back. She had a genius for packing things that amazed Lazarus.

The Innruld strode over like an angry stork, clipboard in hand like he might use it as a sword.

One impossibly-long finger tracked down the inventory until he found the note he wanted, confronting Lazarus like an angry chipmunk.

"That box supposedly weighs one hundred and seventeen pounds, human," he demanded, maybe of the gods.

"Sounds about right," Lazarus replied sullenly with a placid nod.

He wasn't supposed to be enjoying the games Aileen was playing with the man.

The Innruld set the clipboard atop the box and squatted down, apparently intent on proving them all liars by showing they had packed it light. Smugglers, maybe.

Except the boxes Aileen was concerned about were on her

side, bottom row, outside facing, second and fifth from the front.

The Innruld grunted. Grunted again.

"Open this crate," he ordered, storking back up to his seven feet and change.

Lazarus glanced at the man's boots and nearly giggled when he saw the three-inch heels the being effected.

*Yeah, I got your number, buddy.*

"Uh, Aileen?" Lazarus looked around blankly.

"We don't have the authority to open the box, or even a tool," she lied facilely up at the stupid bird of an Innruld Customs Official. "Shipper sealed at origin. The paperwork for a box opened before delivery will take a considerable amount of time to fill out."

"I will handle that myself," the man growled peevishly, which Lazarus found rather impressive.

Lazarus was taken aback by the man's voice. Innruld sounded generally like humans, with the man speaking normally in a low tenor, but rage drove him up the scale like a bird.

Lazarus turned into a second bass when he was that angry.

"You, get the necessary tools," the officer snapped at one of the guards. Not the Kreeghal.

Everybody stood around and watched as the being scampered off on reverse-hinged, bony legs that reminded Lazarus of a running chicken, as compared to the boss that looked like a mad, wet hen right now. Eventually, the being returned with a thing that looked like an oversized socket wrench, two feet long and nickel-plated with a star-torque-style head.

The one Aileen had hidden in the engine rooms was half again longer and matte black, but scuffed and scarred far more than this pretty thing.

The guard handed the tool to the officer, who thrust it at Lazarus.

"Open it," he ordered.

"Uhm, how?" Lazarus looked up at the man blankly.

"What do you mean, how?" the man howled like a lonely coyote on a cold night.

"He's never seen or used one of these tools, Your Grace," Aileen stepped around the sled and put on her best simper.

Lazarus had wondered how such apparent rebellion among the non-Innruld could survive and thrive, but he had been thinking in human terms. Humans got *mean* in situations like this. This person had never been thwarted in his life, so *flustered* was the order of the day.

Mad, wet, hen.

"You do it, then," the officer snapped.

For the briefest instant, Lazarus saw a smile flash by on the Kreeghal's face when he thought nobody was looking.

So, even their loyalists recognized absurdity. Good to know.

Lazarus stepped back and watched as Aileen slotted the head into a hole and adjusted it just so. She stepped back and gestured Lazarus forward.

"Hold and lift to unbolt the mechanism," she ordered him.

Like he had never opened such a box to check the contents before.

Lazarus gripped it with one hand and braced his feet, understanding that he needed to put on a show now. Rather than grunt and twist, like he was loosening lug nuts, he flexed an arm-wrestling move and heard the bolt squeak in protest as it opened.

Again, jaws dropping open. Like maybe Aileen would have had to climb under the tool and drive upward with all her strength, if she didn't have to resort to an impact hammer.

Those bolts would normally probably defeat casual strength. This one was barely more than finger-tight.

Aileen stopped his motion and moved the tool to the next corner bolt. All four gave up fairly quickly, and Lazarus lifted the lid off the box with his fingers and stepped out of the way.

The Customs officer pulled a smaller box from the interior. The brand name on the side made no sense to Lazarus, but it was pretty heavy and this crate had been holding machine parts and tools shipped from some central factory to the boonies.

Eventually, the whole box was emptied onto the deck, inspected disdainfully with a sniff and then packed again. Lazarus knew he'd have never gotten them to fit, but Aileen had apparently memorized the pattern and recreated it perfectly.

Awesome to watch.

"Close it up," Aileen ordered him bluntly. "The officer and I must now fill out all the paperwork for a container that has lost the shipper's seal."

Lazarus had a hard time containing the juvenile giggles when she turned to the Innruld officer with an innocent smile.

"Unless there are other boxes here we should open?" she asked. "Each set of papers will take about an hour to fill out, so this sled should only take us three days, if we don't sleep."

Both of the guards snorted under their breaths. The Innruld crimsoned beautifully and then snarled in perfect silence as he realized that she was going to require the paperwork.

He had insisted. And those were the rules.

"Here," the man practically slapped Lazarus on the chest with the clipboard as he turned away.

Lazarus watched them get about fifteen feet away, the Innruld striding like an angry stork and forcing everyone else to run to keep up.

"Your Grace, you forgot your prybar," Lazarus called innocently, causing the whole party to stop, and the one guard to race madly back and take it from his hands.

Eventually, Lazarus and Remahle were alone in the bay as the outer door closed.

Remahle started giggling so hard that Lazarus was afraid he might fall off his stool.

He did, but the Kr'mari were gliders, so he landed on his feet anyway.

"Priceless," Remahle managed to gasp out before the next wave of giggles.

Lazarus smiled.

"Now what?" he asked.

"Oh, she'll absolutely hold his feet to the fire for that paperwork," Remahle laughed. "She owes him from other trips to Aceanx. In about an hour or so, they'll be back, and the next inspection will be mostly counting boxes, unless something has gone wrong."

"What would happen then?" Lazarus asked nervously.

"Then they'd hang us good."

# CHAPTER TWENTY-FIVE

## LAZARUS

CIVILIAN DOCKS WERE nothing like the military versions Lazarus was used to. At least in Innruld space. But he also had no reason to doubt the similarities, were he to return to Brasilia Prime Station with Aileen and Wybert and the rest for a night of drinking.

Or, in this case, a semi-raucous tea room. The locals were in the middle of what Lazarus interpreted as an improvisational poetry slam as they got seated in a back corner, with Lazarus in a chair that was probably held in storage for any Innruld that might arrive. His feet swung, but that was okay. Aileen's chair came with a small ladder she climbed to get up to table level and Wybert had a nest like would hold a burrito in the microwave.

The show on the floor was mesmerizing. A Vaadwig and a—what? It, she, was centaur-like in the same way that Wybert was, with an upright torso and horizontal lower half that had four feet down. Except she had fur and claws and looked like a spotted leopard in the parts of her fur that weren't covered in a blousy, silk shirt in white that made her golden bits glow.

And Lazarus had never considered how a leotaur tailor might construct shorts until now. Four short pant legs for her, and then buttons down her left side of the…what did you call the long part? Torso was the upright. Stomach? Ribs? Abdomen? Something he had never needed to know before now and didn't want to ask until later.

And she wore sandals that were open-claw, but protected all of her pads while looking stylish in red leather straps.

Female, if the standard design including breasts on the top part of the torso was followed, although he also wondered if putting them underneath like a cow made more sense.

Not even remotely the question to pose.

The Vaadwig woman looked positively dowdy by comparison, in a loose, gray shirt that buttoned up the front and a skirt that more resembled a tabard, split into three panels to fit around her legs and tail.

But they were warriors from the sound. It had apparently been open mic night in the tea shop. The crowd was heavy, but everyone was standing closer to the stage to watch the two women duel, in a manner where each completed a verse that riffed on the other's.

Cheers, jeers, and whistles filled the air.

Lazarus just sat and absorbed it, sipping at his tea and trying to figure out how the drink was made. Dried leaves ground up and immersed in hot water was apparently a universal thing, but then you started to add spices. Aileen had assured him that everything that went into it was something Lazarus had tried safely before.

In a multi-species tea shop, he supposed that detailed and public ingredient lists were an absolute requirement. Don't want to accidentally poison your guests. Bad for the business reputation.

So he watched.

The leotaur woman seemed to be winning, almost dancing with the internal rhythm of her words as she spat them out, rolling her voice from almost a high baritone up to a low soprano that cut the through crowd noise like a diamond blade.

The end came so quickly that Lazarus missed it. The Vaadwig apparently conceded defeat, more or less gracefully, and the crowd settled down to just clapping and stomping. He watched the two women hug once and then jump down into the mob to be surrounded and congratulated by their supporters.

"You have anything like this back home?" Aileen asked as the noise became low enough to talk without yelling.

"I'm not even sure what that was," he said simply. "Except that some musicals frequently have a dance battle at the climax."

"Dance battle?" Wybert's face had almost collapsed in on itself, so hard was he scowling with all five eyes and both the outer four and inner two mandibles.

"Imagine the standard adventure fantasy story," Lazarus tried to explain. "Culminating in the great battle where the hero kills the villain and rescues the princess."

"You people are weird," Aileen noted dryly before she grinned and almost rolled her eyes.

"Agreed, but the forms go back to the Iron Age, so I can't argue with it," Lazarus grinned back and then turned to Wybert. "With me so far?"

"Indeed, after some translation into something that makes more sense," the Ilount replied. "We men must achieve great things to impress a nest queen, so we can mate with her. Slaying terrible villains falls under that rubric."

"Okay, so in a more modern setting, you take the same story, but they are not fighting with weapons," Lazarus said. "Instead, each side takes a turn dancing to show their grace and skill. Eventually, the two leaders of the sides duel, and of course the hero has the better moves. It is the same with many martial arts vids, although there the combat is more violent and deadly. Still, you must present great skill. Great *fu*."

"Seriously, Lazarus, are all humans this crazy?" Aileen asked with a raised eyebrow that finally drifted into the perfect eyeroll while he watched.

"I'm positively boring," he grinned at her. "I can't wait to introduce you to some of the people I know back home."

It was like a light switch had been flipped off. Her face got serious. Lazarus also felt serious take hold of him. The room around them seemed to fall into one of those periodic silences you got at a party.

Even Wybert sobered.

"You think Addison would do it?" she asked in little more than a whisper. "Go to Brasilia with a cargo?"

Lazarus felt a chill wrap icy fingers around his chest. Dare he allow that? Would it help the Rio Alliance?

On the one hand, his people could suddenly call on a lot of people who didn't think human supremacy was the key to galactic development. Conversely, how quickly would the Innruld object and get involved?

Did Lazarus really want responsibility for perhaps unleashing a galaxy-wide war between species on his conscience? Because both the Innruld and Westphalia would get ugly before they settled it. Of that, Lazarus had no doubts. Supreme power never willingly surrenders itself. Some places had historically been willing to share power on ethical and moral grounds, but usually it required some level of violent revolution.

Like, say, the Rio Alliance issuing a declaration of independence from Westphalia.

*Quando no curso de eventos humanos…*

*When in the course of human events…*

"I don't know, Aileen," Lazarus finally said, having run any number of scenarios through his head in the silence that had faded around them as tea shop noise rose up again. "We still have your mission to Zhoonarrim first. After that, I'm not sure what Addison will want to do."

"Will you stay with the ship after that?" Wybert asked, almost comically insecure in his tones. Hurt at even the possibility that Lazarus might move on, after the month or so serving with them.

Lazarus knew he had gotten lucky in being captured by Addison Wolcott and *Shiva Zephyr Glaive.* He could have just as easily been penned like a zoo animal, or tortured for information that might have given someone else an unmatchable edge in this space.

Especially if the star drives on *Ajax* were something so far advanced over Innruld Space that he could upset everyone's apple cart.

And then there were the guns.

Addison had shown him a patrol vessel overseen by the overlords of space. They had ray shielding, but it wasn't nearly as hard as an equivalent Rio warship's. Or Westphalian. Would Westphalia's navy roll over Innruld space if they came this far?

The Security Barc didn't seem to mount anything bigger than a Star Spear, for destructive power, and only a few of those, relying mostly on Power Bolts, usually in twinned or tripled turrets.

Good for banging on freighters. Might tickle *Ajax*'s ray shields if he sat there and let them.

"I have to see what Addison has planned," Lazarus temporized, looking at each of them in turn. "His next cargo might be taking him deeper into Innruld Space, when I need to see if I can find a way home. I don't have money to buy my own vessel and just sail there."

"What's Brasilia like?" Aileen asked suddenly.

Normally, she was the shy one in most crew settings, so Lazarus was taken briefly aback.

"Crowded," he said. "Population around four billion people, with over eighty percent of that being human."

"Four billion?" Wybert goggled. "On one world?"

"Greenbriar, the capital city, has a population of about fourteen million," Lazarus said. "Most of the non-humans live close by, so the population split is closer to fifty/fifty."

"How do you fit that many people on a world?" Aileen joined Wybert in shock. "Or a city? There are whole colonies I know with fewer sentients."

"Greenbriar is a city of towers," Lazarus said. "Towering arcologies in a variety of shapes, although nothing like Skycity above us. Vast amount of land are given over to fields to grow crops."

"Still, what is the population of the Rio Alliance?" Aileen asked timorously.

"All total?" Lazarus leaned back and Aileen nodded. "Probably about forty billion sentients. Westphalia is five times that, but they have many more worlds."

Dead shock. Mouths fallen open. Whites of eyes.

Lazarus wondered what he had missed in his studies. Then it dawned on him. All of Innruld Space was physically larger than Westphalia, for worlds, but they were less densely populated. The whole of this Space probably had about one hundred billion sentients in it, but Rio and Westphalia were all human, for the most part.

Innruld Space had at least forty species as members. Just splitting that remotely evenly suggested maybe five billion of one species, living thinly on their worlds and in space, more in harmony with the land.

And easily, utterly dominated by the Innruld overlords, culturally, socially, and financially.

Humans arriving here would be like a nest of fire ants deciding to move into your back yard. They came and did whatever they wanted, and you just hoped that they didn't decide to wipe you out or push you off the land.

"Oh," Lazarus saw the truth. "We can't tell the Rio Alliance about this place. Humans would overwhelm you in a generation."

"How fast do your kind breed?" Aileen asked in a dry voice.

"Prodigiously, when necessary," Lazarus replied. "One child per mother per year or two for a stretch of ten or fifteen years is not unheard of on new colony worlds."

"Ten children in fifteen years?" Wybert's mandibles flexed all the way open like a flower for a moment before snapping shut. "Every female human? Not even a queen?"

Lazarus knew that motion to be shock so great that Wybert had lost control of the muscles in his face.

A commotion nearby drew Lazarus's attention. The room had fallen dead silent in ways it had not achieved even when the poetry slam was reaching its crescendo.

Seven Innruld had entered. Five of them were male, and two female. Well dressed in the height of fashion, from what Lazarus had learned. Towering over the rest of the room by two feet or more.

All eyes had turned to this table. Every head in the entire establishment.

The air had a charge like lightning was about to strike. Even Wybert noticed it.

Lazarus glowered back at the intruders just as hard as they stared this way.

The man in the middle of the social circle had a woman

on his arm, as did one other. Three looked more like friends than bodyguards. They began to walk this way.

Lazarus considered weapons, but there were none. You didn't go armed on station. Even Wybert's powerspear was stashed just inside the airlock for when he got home.

The round table was metal. Thin and relatively light. Four feet across on four legs. Cheap to haul to orbit for its strength. It would make a useful battering ram or shield in a pinch.

The chair he was seated on was wood. Elaborately carved and delicate, he had been afraid it might crack under his weight, but the men approaching all weighed roughly the same as he did. Just stretched an extra foot.

None of them looked like sailors. Fops in lace, seeing the cuffs peeking out from several jackets. The two women looked like high-bred aristocrats in the mold that Westphalia turned out, rather than working girls who might know how to take care of themselves in these sorts of rougher neighborhoods.

Lazarus slid forward on the chair until his feet hit the deck and he had a grip.

"What, pray tell, is this pitiful creature that sits in my chair?" the leader asked the room in a theatrical, almost melodramatic voice.

"Human," Lazarus replied simply. "What species are you?"

Up close, those eyes weren't blue-gold anymore. Something had changed them to a hard azure that almost glowed in the tea shop's normal dimness. All of them were like that, to one degree or another. None of them had normal eyes, at least for an Innruld.

Lazarus wondered if they had consumed some narcotic chemical before entering an area that wasn't necessarily off-limits to the Innruld, but certainly not their normal cup of tea.

"We are Innruld, pipsqueak," the leader growled. "Your betters."

"Really?" Lazarus smiled harshly at the man. "I don't seem to remember getting that memo."

He was aware that he had an audience consisting of most of the tea shop, on a night when an open mic poetry slam battle had the place nearly full. Wybert was practically vibrating with suppressed energy, but Lazarus had no idea if an Ilount was a match for even one Innruld, despite his greater mass and extra arms.

Lazarus grinned at the thought of a martial arts master from Greenbriar inventing a new form of Kung Fu to teach a decapeed with four arms. His own military training had included some level of unarmed close combat training, but nothing like Wybert might need.

"Get up, human," the Innruld snarled in an ugly voice.

The room seemed poised. Lazarus didn't dare look around, but the other six invaders were all in front of him in a compact knot, like maybe they didn't dare let the crowd get behind them if trouble started.

After all, when was likely the last time someone told a man like this *No*?

Lazarus pretended to study his options for several seconds.

"No. No, I don't think so. I was here first. You can find someplace else to drink," he spoke up to the man, and then let his face harden and his voice drop. "Or somewhere else to go."

He hadn't read the legal statutes involved, but Lazarus did know that there was a world of difference between starting a brawl and merely defending yourself from one. Back home, the time-honored tradition had gotten translated as the Texas Defense, after a region of harsh deserts located on Earth.

*"Yer Honor, he needed killing."*

Except that killing the man would cause more troubles when there were many layers of violence short of that, when dealing with what Lazarus assumed was a drunk bully, however the man had gotten himself into this state.

The leader of the little tribe of outsiders muttered a curse under his breath and stepped clear of the small group. A hand like spiderweb descended on Lazarus's shoulder and tried to pull him off the chair.

Lazarus braced his feet and smiled evenly at the man, unwilling to cede.

The man pushed next, a move telegraphed by hands, feet, and head. It had no effect either, other than causing the Innruld to grunt with useless effort.

The next move surprised Lazarus, but only briefly.

The idiot slapped him.

Open palm to the left cheek. Resounding crack that would have been audible even over the noise of a poetry slam. Sting, but nothing all that impressive.

The room gasped in unison.

A much younger Lazarus, when he had a different name, had been slapped harder by an angry woman. He had still gone into the military and the rest of his life, rather than remain behind with her.

"You know," Lazarus spoke almost conversationally, given the silence, "where I come from, that's a method used to issue a formal challenge. Usually a duel with lethal weapons between the aggressor and the aggrieved. Do you wish to do me personal violence, sir?"

Another gasp. Apparently nobody had ever talked back to folks like this. Maybe this particular person, even. He looked like a punk-ass bully.

Then the idiot made a mistake. In retrospect, a predictable one, but a mistake nonetheless.

He went for a backhand.

Lazarus caught it before it landed. Wrapped his long fingers around that tiny wrist that felt like a ten-year-old's. Squeezed just a little. Twisted inward towards the thumb, in the direction no arm likes to turn.

Idiot rotated with his arm in a locked arm bar, suddenly facing his little mob of dancers, surrounded by the galaxy's meanest-looking poetry mob.

Lazarus rose from his chair now, so he could continue twisting as the man tried to evade. One hand to keep the elbow straight. The other pulling it up until the man had the option of a dislocated shoulder or surrendering his height advantage.

One of the Innruld men raised a clenched fist and took a step forward.

Lazarus let go of Idiot One and punched Two in what he hoped was the softest part of the belly. No time to calculate the locations of internal organs he had studied previously. Just a belly punch in a bar fight.

Damn it, he was too old to keep getting into this sort of thing.

Two folded over the fist with a tremendous whooooooosh of air and collapsed. Three took a stutter step forward, as if to do something, so Lazarus poked him square in the middle of the chest with a fist. Not trying to break anything, fearful of bird bones on these people, but hard enough that Three landed on his butt after several comical windmill steps backwards.

One of the Innruld women turned and snarled at him. She had been on One's arm earlier.

"I'll hit a woman." Lazarus promised her with the sort of lethal cold you found in the darkness between stars.

She was either less stoned than the men, or smarter. She nodded ever so slightly and stepped back.

Lazarus decided that he couldn't really win the fight the way his first military instructor would have preferred. A dead Innruld, his head shattered all over the floor, would make one hell of a powerful statement, but he'd end up in jail, or executed.

Instead, Lazarus grabbed a handful of that pretty, blond hair that they all seemed to have. One's was longer than any of the others', so Lazarus got a good grip and pulled the man to his feet, and then kept him doubled over by dragging him to the front door and judo-tossing the Innruld over one hip.

He was just sorry that they were on a station, so there were no mud puddles for that pretty set of clothes to absorb.

The other six had remained frozen in place when Lazarus turned, so he beckoned them silently, his eyes promising painful mayhem if he had to come in there to get them.

The leader's woman walked first, head upright and frozen on the distant horizon so she didn't have to see the faces around her as she made her exit. The second woman drug her beau along in the first's wake.

Lazarus locked eyes on the one still standing and smiled like a wolf coming over a rise at a wounded traveler. That fellow wisely helped his buddy to that being's feet and they stumbled out of the poetry slam to giggles and cat-calls.

Lazarus waited for them to exit and smiled at the woman who seemed to be in charge now.

"Wait here, and I'll retrieve your friend," he promised.

Inside, nobody had moved, not even the normally aggressive Wybert of Capantzina. Lazarus grabbed the unconscious Innruld by collar and belt buckle and thrust himself into a fireman's carry, like they did every year for evacuation training on a warship. This fool was lighter than some of the dummies Lazarus had been required to carry.

Two went into the corridor next to One, who was just now starting to regain his senses on the deck.

Lazarus fixed the woman with a hard stare for a moment.

"I dare not suggest that you and your friends are not welcome here," he said with a cold sneer. "But perhaps you might impress better manners on your friends, should you decide to return someday. I'm willing to ignore his challenge and not send my seconds around to bring this fool to the dueling ground. I doubt he'd last ten seconds with a blade against me, and I have the choice of weapons. Keep that in mind, should you decide to send gendarmes or bullyboys after me. Humans aren't fearful, little minions of the Innruld like some other species."

The species was normally pale by comparison, an ethereal, icy beauty that made them almost mobile art installations. Even more so tonight with those eyes that seemed to glow with internal fire from whatever drugs or substances they had ingested.

She was the color of fresh snow right now.

Lazarus looked over the others with a sneer fit for the gods before returning to the tea shop. He sat back down in the chair that had apparently represented so much honor and authority before the slightest whisper broke the room.

"In three minutes, we should probably find a back way out of here and run like hell to the ship." He looked earnestly at Aileen. "I don't know if they're smart enough to call my bluff, but we're already loaded for Zhoonarrim, so maybe we should convince Addison to take off before those folks can send trouble after us."

"You think they will?" Wybert asked. "You just handled seven of them by yourself."

"That's exactly why I think they will," Lazarus said. "Nobody has had a reason to fear my kind before tonight."

# CHAPTER TWENTY-SIX

ADDISON

ADDISON STARED at the two like he was seeing complete strangers on his deck, and not his longtime Loadmaster and her new human assistant. Wybert had taken up what Addison could only quantify as guard duty at the airlock hatch, with that stupid powerspear of his in two hands, ready to fend off hordes of police.

One scaly hand went up to rub against a sudden pain in his left temple, above and behind the bone ridge. Aileen and Lazarus sat perfectly still across the desk with the door to his office closed.

"Seven of them?" he asked, still trying to come to terms with the potential bounds of human violence.

If there were any.

"Three," Lazarus replied. "One at a time. Punks with superiority complexes and no training at all. Sailors would have known how to handle themselves."

"Human sailors, perhaps," Aileen chimed in for the first time since completing her story. "How violent are your kind?"

Addison watched the human start to react to the Yithadreph woman, pause, and then shrug.

"I'm beginning to suspect moreso than folks around here," he finally admitted in a rueful tone.

It wasn't a topic that had come up before, other than an admission that the human had belonged to an organized military, something Innruld space didn't understand. It apparently included close combat training. In addition to size, bulk, and weight.

Lazarus had, Addison knew, been at great pains to be calm and self-contained around the crew. Kuei had finally gotten around to mentioning to Addison the setup in the shower.

Addison wasn't sure at this point that the three of them could have prevented the human from doing something that day, had he been inclined, based on this new information. Wybert was as close to a warrior as Addison knew, and he doubted the Ilount would ever impress a queen.

Addison opened a line to the bridge.

"Cormac, is everyone aboard?" he asked.

"*Affirmative, Director,*" the NavCrawler replied immediately. "*Aileen, Wybert, and Lazarus had the last station rotation, since they were busy with cargo when you let the others have time.*"

"File a flight plan immediately," Addison decided. "Sudden priority cargo, if they ask, and get us launched and clear of the station as soon as the gates open wide enough that we're not facing fines. Let Kuei know."

"*Immediately, Director,*" Cormac said.

Addison settled back on his coil and studied the human. Bipeds blushed. At least humans shared that with many of them.

"How much trouble have I just caused you, sir?" the human sounded abashed.

"That depends on who those children were," Addison replied. "And how embarrassed or frightened they were when they got back to Skycity. If one of them was the scion of a notable family, they might register a complaint and try to take you into custody. I'm sure the tea shop has video of everything, especially if it was a poetry slam night, plus all manner of witnesses. If it happened as Aileen described it, you're facing a fine at most, but your name will go on a list."

"Not the first time that's happened, sir," Lazarus managed to sound proud and embarrassed at the same time.

"Oh?"

"I wasn't always a Captain, sir," he said. "A Director of a warship. Before that I was a rowdy kid junior officer."

"Troublesome?" Addison asked.

"Let's just say that fifteen years since have turned me into several different people from the dumb punk I used to be?" Lazarus smiled wryly.

Addison nodded.

"We'll probably need to stay away from Aceanx for a time," Addison noted. "And hope that nobody here decides to pursue a vendetta to Zhoonarrim."

"And after Zhoonarrim, sir?" Lazarus asked.

"Why do you ask, Lazarus?" Addison felt something start to pain his temple again, but he sat still and concentrated on relaxing the muscles from his waist up in bands around his middle. Rubbing his forehead ridges wouldn't help.

"A conversation Aileen and I were having just before the trouble broke out."

The human glanced over at the Yithadreph for some sort of permission.

Apparently he got it, because he nodded and looked back at his director for a long second.

"The population of Innruld Space is around one hundred billion sentients, sir?" Lazarus said.

"Conservatively, yes," Addison agreed.

"The Rio Alliance worlds are a little less than half that, combined," the human's lips pinched in on themselves in an interesting manner. "Westphalia is about double Innruld, all things organized."

"Two hundred billion?" Addison felt his breath catch. Aileen almost cringed.

"Yes, so combined we're probably looking at two hundred billion humans in my sectors of space once you filter out the other species, Addison," Lazarus said. "It registered on me, when Aileen asked, that humans also breed at a much higher rate than most other species. Your single largest population in Innruld Space by species is probably ten to twelve billion. And that's all the various sub-species of Churquen combined."

Addison nodded, then felt his eyeslits fall open to their widest as the implications hit him.

Two hundred billion humans? Fast breeding? Aggressive?

"Shit," he managed to mutter.

Aileen nodded. So did Lazarus.

"I know the crew has gossiped about whether you would take *Shiva Zephyr Glaive* and set out for human space after Zhoonarrim, Addison," Lazarus dropped his voice down into the personal and conspiratorial. "I'm not sure that that's a good idea. My kind might quickly overwhelm you on sheer numbers."

Addison nodded. Lazarus had thought to set himself up as a guardian of his new friends, against the might of two much larger places. It was a perfectly ethical solution, to hide Innruld space from the humans.

It was also doomed to utter failure.

"Won't work," Addison said, watching the human's face as emotions played out around his eyes and chin, much like on a Churquen.

"It won't?" Aileen spoke up, surprised by Addison's response.

"It will not," Addison stated firmly. "Suppose that neither Rio Alliance or Westphalia chance to come in this direction anytime soon. How much worse will it be when it does happen, centuries from now?"

"Oh," Lazarus had a moment of insight. "How long have you have trans-space?"

Addison paused to think about it.

"The Qooph first discovered it about five thousand years ago," he said. "Their explorations found others at various levels of industrial technology and uplifted them. I'm surprised the humans weren't found then."

"Five thousand years ago, humans had just started using written records and had not yet moved beyond bronze technology, Addison. We've been out in the galaxy for barely seven hundred years."

Addison felt his jaw drop open again. It might become an occupational hazard, at this rate. But he held to his logic. It was still sound.

"Better then, absolutely, that we discover each other now," Addison said. "While the Rio Alliance welcomes non-humans and needs help against Westphalia. Where will you likely be in a century?"

"Perhaps another twenty or forty billion humans, as we continue to expand," Lazarus nodded in recognition. "So many worlds already have atmospheres that can be modified easily. Human crops and biomes can be delivered, and we can move in fast enough to make them more earth-like. What about your superiors?"

So, he had made that leap of logic. Had understood that Addison Wolcott was an agent of shadowy others, and not just a drug runner fighting his own personal war against the Innruld.

Not just.

"What about them?" Addison asked. "I own this ship. They assign me missions that I am free to skip, if I feel the risk is too great."

"Will they want me killed before I can get home and let the humans know about you?" Lazarus asked. "Will they hear the stories of that bar and suddenly fear me more than the Innruld? Better the devil you know that the one you don't?"

Now it was Addison's turn to think.

He had approached it from the standpoint that any delay worked in the human's favor, over the next thousand years. Would Eha and her superiors understand that logic, or panic when they learned this painful, new truth?

What manner of nastiness might they find when they got to Zhoonarrim, not just from Lazarus's enemies, but also people who might suddenly become Addison's?

But there was really only one way to handle this. Rip the scab off right now and deal with the issue, while it might still be compact enough to handle. A century from now, humans might have expanded to another thirty or fifty star systems, if that growth rate was to be believed.

Why had his people never done the same?

But Addison knew the answer to that.

Innruld.

The overlords had maneuvered themselves into a position of authority two thousand years ago and set up the three-tiered hierarchy that Addison and Eha and others had dedicated themselves to undoing.

Innruld overlords controlling wealth and political power by co-opting the dangerous, seducing them with money and then either blunting them, or destroying them.

The armed tier. All those guards, bureaucrats, and servants from other species that accepted the wealth and prestige they got from keeping a boot on the throats of their own kind for the masters.

And the rabble. Addison Wolcott and friends. Underground rebellions. Piratical gangs. Men and women in the street just trying to get by, maybe making enough to take a vacation this year to a semi-exotic resort off-planet.

How do you convince people to throw off the chains they have come to define themselves by?

"How dangerous are you as a warrior on a dock, Lazarus?" Addison asked, getting right to the heart of the next station's problems.

"How dangerous is Wybert?" the human volleyed back earnestly.

"About in the middle," Aileen spoke up. "Better than some. Worse than others. Not a hero. Not a failure. Never a breeder, most likely."

"Then I'm probably closer to the top than I realized," Lazarus said. "When we arrived, the Innruld had a guard with him. Three eyes. Squat and powerful, with short legs and long arms. I think he was a Kreeghal."

"He was," Aileen agreed.

"I would not want to Greco-Roman wrestle with one of his kind," Lazarus admitted. "Probably tie me into a knot without a lot of effort. With any sort of melee weapons, however, that's a whole different story."

The way he said that last made Addison's tailtip twitch. Fortunately, it was hidden inside his coil, so nobody noticed. He was studying the human's face. Saw the depth of potential violence his kind apparently just took for granted.

"What kind of weapon are you thinking about?" Addison had to inquire. "Wybert's spear?"

"No," Lazarus shook his head. "Too obvious. Maybe a sap or a length of pipe about as long as my forearm."

"Sap?" Aileen's face was as scrunched up as Addison wouldn't allow his to become.

"Small bag, made of either leather or a heavy cloth." Lazarus held up his palm as if cupping a ball. "Maybe a pound of sand or lead dropshot inside. Generally not a lethal weapon in a fight."

*Generally not a lethal weapon in a fight?*

Not for the first time, Addison wondered if his greed had overcome his sense. Eha might agree, by the time he saw her again at Zhoonarrim, and he had no doubts about that coming event.

But greed was all that kept him from having the human killed. Locked in his quarters with the life support cut until he suffocated, perhaps. Poison in his food. Something.

*Ajax* was out there. Addison had come to hang his hopes on that vessel, wherever it was.

He just hoped it wasn't leading him and his entire species unto death.

"At Zhoonarrim, you can defend yourself," Addison decided. "Non-lethally. Most likely, nobody will even care who you are, so I won't confine you to the ship, but stay away from fights if you want to remain a crewmember. Am I understood?"

"Perfectly, sir," Lazarus said. "I've given almost the identical speech myself."

Yes, he probably had. Being a Director was a universal thing, regardless of species.

"Dismissed," Addison sent them on their way with no more glower than the headache behind his eyes that stubbornly refused to leave.

At least he was being honest with himself he hoped, as they left him alone in his office. His greed had the potential to overthrow the Innruld, either in the form of an alien warship, or the sudden availability of a new species that outnumbered everyone else in space and might *hopefully* be friendly.

Against the risk that the Rio Alliance panicked at the discovery of Innruld Space and made common cause with Westphalia to conquer a thousand new worlds and simply replace the Innruld as the ruling class for the galaxy.

The dice had been cast.

# CHAPTER TWENTY-SEVEN

## LAZARUS

"WHAT IS the purpose of this tool?" a deep voice intruded on Lazarus as he worked, so oblivious to the world that someone had snuck up on him.

He glanced up and saw only the wall of the primary cargo bay in front of him, dominated by the latest stacks of cargo that Aileen had caused him to rearrange, adding capacity when he could do things easily that the rest of the crew could not.

Movement on his left drew his eye. Ereshkiki Nisab, the Qooph Systems Mechanic, a blue-gray wheel of polished marble with arms coming out of the axle on both sides and six eyes and six mouths around the inner circumference of the twin rims.

Lazarus had been so focused, so lost inside himself, that the Qooph had rolled right up and settled on a deflated hex facing.

Sounded about right.

He held up the thing in his hands. Leather. About seven inches long and wide enough to wrap around his left forearm like a bracer. Aluminum plate from ship's stores had been cut into strips, and Lazarus was almost done gluing them individually to the backing leather. Thadrakho had promised that his sewing machine had the necessary torque to punch through the leather that would wrap both ends and seam the design.

"It is a secret, Ereshkiki Nisab," Lazarus replied, making contact with the central eye on this side. "A shield I can wear under my shirt."

How did you tell which eye to look at, if three of them could all turn your way from different parts of the rim?

"Shield?"

"It will go around my left arm, strapped tight and hidden under my shirt sleeves," Lazarus continued.

"Again, what is the purpose of this tool?" the Qooph pressed.

"If someone attacks me with a knife, I can block them without being cut," Lazarus replied, letting some of the seriousness out of his soul. "Similarly, if they swing a club, it will not break my arm if they hit me there."

The talk with Addison had left him more off balance than he had realized until now.

"You expect violence at Zhoonarrim?" Ereshkiki Nisab asked.

"I do not know, Ereshkiki Nisab," Lazarus finally admitted. "Humans would probably bring some level of vendetta from Aceanx. This is not a weapon, so I fulfill my promise to Addison to only defend myself if attacked. And if the authorities arrest me, again, I am not technically armed under Innruld law."

"You think the overlords will come for you?" Ereshkiki Nisab seemed surprised by the concept.

Lazarus shrugged, and then wondered what a Qooph might do to convey the same emotion. They had no shoulders, as the arms that reminded him of a cat's tail, ending in six, opposed fingers, just emerged from the axle, and the central body was two, hex-shaped ribcages of struts holding everything up. Round when everything was inflated to roll.

All the internals of a Qooph were pockets and tubes that connected eyes or stomachs to centralized organs.

"I do not know the truth of your worlds, Ereshkiki Nisab," Lazarus added. "My own are a much more violent, dangerous place, and I fear that my kind will harm you and yours when we eventually meet. For now, I need to protect myself against reprisals by bullies hiding behind authority, and later I can serve as an ambassador."

"Addison has told me about your worlds," Ereshkiki Nisab noted. "It is possible that one of my great-grandsires visited your Earth in the ancient times. But for the Innruld, we might have returned as you developed, and joined you with galactic civilization ere now."

"Your great-grandsire?" Lazarus felt his mouth fall open. "How long do Qooph live normally?"

"Twelve to fifteen centuries, if nothing goes wrong," the wheelman replied, blinking with what Lazarus felt conveyed amusement. "You ephemerals are endlessly fascinating to watch and know."

Lazarus suddenly felt like a particularly bright dog, contemplating how many generations of humans this Qooph might know in the sequence of his lifetime.

"Do you have records?" Lazarus asked. "I meant to inquire later, but now is as good a time as any."

"Not written archives," Ereshkiki Nisab rumbled after a moment. "The Innruld do not permit those records, but the Elders of the Wide Road might have the oral tales, slowly handing them down."

*The Innruld do not permit those records.*

Lazarus found a deep and abiding hatred of the so-called

overlords flare up, though he hoped he kept it hidden. How much did that species control the rest by not allowing certain information to be free? By erasing their past?

What would these sectors of space be like if all species were largely equal, as the Rio Alliance was trying to build?

"At some point, I think it would be useful to know," Lazarus managed through gritted teeth. "Some of our oldest written tales describe a being, an Angel sent by God, who bore a remarkable resemblance to a Qooph, depending on how you translate certain terms."

"Indeed?" the eyes seemed to open wider.

"Ezekiel One," Lazarus nodded.

> As for the appearance of the wheels and their
> construction: their appearance was like
> the gleaming of beryl. And the four had
> the same likeness, their appearance and
> construction being as it were a wheel
> within a wheel. When they went, they
> went in any of their four directions
> without turning as they went. And their
> rims were tall and awesome, and the rims
> of all four were full of eyes all around.
> And when the living creatures went, the
> wheels went beside them; and when the
> living creatures rose from the earth, the
> wheels rose. Wherever the spirit wanted
> to go, they went, and the wheels rose
> along with them, for the spirit of the
> living creatures was in the wheels.

Lazarus let his eyes come back to the present and studied the Qooph in front of him.

"If you had a spherical land craft within which you could

roll, pivoting yourself as needed, that might be you," he intoned.

"And we have used such things, back in the distant past, Lazarus," Ereshkiki Nisab replied with a delight in his voice. "How interesting to think that the memory of Qooph explorers might have survived on Earth. I will inquire when next I am among my kind."

Lazarus didn't ask when that might be. As long-lived as the Qooph were, it might be decades. Or there might be an elder at Zhoonarrim. He had no way to guess.

"So you are preparing to defend yourself against violence?" Ereshkiki Nisab pivoted the entire conversation back to the start. "But not to harm others?"

"If I can, I will turn the other cheek," Lazarus said. "But I am not above claiming an eye for an eye, under the older codes. Too much hangs on it."

Like, perhaps, the future history of the entire galaxy.

# CHAPTER TWENTY-EIGHT

## AILEEN

WHATEVER MISGIVINGS she might have had, Aileen had quashed them as the ship entered the inner keep of the Zhoonarrim station. She wasn't violent, but there was the potential for trouble when they landed and had to face the authorities that would be waiting for them.

She hoped that the lurid tales from both Dormell and Aceanx had not yet made it here, so they could just drop off their cargo and figure out what Addison's next move was. The boss had been remarkably tight-lipped about things over the last week, which was never a good sign.

Aileen glanced over at Remahle, wondering if she should have swapped him for Wybert today. The Kr'mari was a better driver of the cargo sled, but the Ilount would at least know what he was doing if things got suddenly bad.

Remahle would probably just run for cover. Aileen felt that she owed Lazarus more than just a wave goodbye if the authorities arrested the human, although she wasn't exactly sure what she could do in that situation.

Around her *Shiva Zephyr Glaive* settled on the landing platform. Felt like number six from the sequence the maneuvering jets had fired. Not the best place to put someone if you wanted a public scene making an arrest. Nor if you were aiming for something quiet.

Hopefully that was a good sign.

Lazarus had been especially tight and quiet the last few days, but she understood. And he had done all the work asked of him without even the laughing complaints that were usual.

Who knew what was about to stick to their fur?

Outside, the bell sound of the airlock doors closing, transmitted through her shoes and legs into her soul. Air would start to flood the outer chamber next, until the customs officials could enter the chamber and begin their usual round of annoying questions.

Addison surprised the hell out of her by slithering into the chamber, wearing his best tunic vest, the dressy red one that reminded people he was a ship's Director.

"Addison?" she asked, at a loss for other words.

"Maybe I'm being paranoid," he replied. "Maybe not. We'll find out shortly."

Lazarus stirred uncomfortably, but remained silent. Aileen wondered if Wybert was hiding just outside the chamber, or over by the main airlock ramp, where he could charge in if the situation demanded.

Maybe the human really was part of the crew now. One of theirs.

"Thank you," Lazarus murmured quietly to Addison.

The Director just nodded and everyone stood around waiting.

The knock came quickly enough. Three metallic bangs on one of the landing legs to indicate that the outer chamber was pressurized.

Addison nodded to her and Aileen triggered the lift to lower them to the deck outside.

First thing that caught her eye was the officer. He was Vaadwig, not Innruld. Probably a good sign.

And he was unarmed, save for the usual two goons that they were issued when they got out of bed in the morning. So, nobody being arrested today, or they didn't warn him how dangerous a human might be if aroused.

Aileen wasn't the only one whose sigh of relief was covered by the sound of the lift clanging into the deck below it.

The Vaadwig officer stepped forward and studied the four of them. She'd dealt with him before, but didn't bother with names. Their kind didn't foster socialization with civilians. He was about in the middle, as bureaucrats went, on the scale of annoying.

"Director," he nodded to Addison, recognizing the man from the years Addison had traveled these docks, even before she had joined his crew.

She and Remahle got looks that summed up bored disdain. Lazarus got a double-take, especially due to his size, but the human just smiled without showing any teeth.

Just another sailor making an honest buck.

"Papers?" the officer demanded.

Aileen handed him the three ID cards she had. Addison added his a moment later. Then the magical clipboard with all the notes about this cargo went into the officer's hands.

"Anything interesting?" the Vaadwig asked, trying to sound companionable from his tone.

"Couple of boxes of medicines for the hospital," Aileen said. "One of them supposedly has radiologicals in it, but sealed up tight in lead for transit, so nothing that has shown up on any handheld scanners to date. Box seven on your list."

One furry finger traced the page, worked its way across. She watched the man mouth the contents silently as he read them. He pulled his own handscanner and pointed it at the sled, waiting several seconds for the output to beep.

The officer nodded to himself, satisfied that the container had not ruptured in flight.

Aileen smiled. Three quarters of smuggling came down to passing the attitude check. Not being nervous or aggressive when questioned. Faking bored, when two of those boxes would get everyone on this ship executed by the Innruld.

No other species was sensitive enough to the materials to ingest them recreationally. This Vaadwig could probably get a better high just over-salting his lunch.

Deflected, the officer pulled out his stamp and inked the middle of the page with a shipping approval.

Aileen smiled up at him.

"Any news on station we should know about?" she asked.

"At the tail end of beyond?" the officer's eyebrows went up. "If you hadn't docked, I might not have left my office except for lunch today."

"Huh," Aileen shrugged. "Business slowing down around here?"

Always useful to know if a slump or recession was coming. Cargo still needed to move around, but the contents would change, even if the actual amount didn't. More things to keep the plebes entertained so they didn't riot over lost jobs and declining lifestyles, especially as the Innruld always seemed insulated against it.

Wealth was a wonderful thing. But only if you had it.

"Maybe a tenth, year over year," the man said absently, handing her back the clipboard.

Aileen glanced over at Addison and caught the gleam in his eyes. Not a good sign, even if Zhoonarrim was kind of in a dead-end pocket as far as cargo transport went.

"Thank you," Aileen said to the Vaadwig's back as he

turned and lumbered off, tail/feet/tail/feet, with his two guards in slow pursuit.

Everybody stood perfectly still until the outer hatch closed.

"Thoughts?" Aileen turned to Addison, watching him and Lazarus both relax by the way their shoulders slumped in unison.

"Shore leave is approved, as soon as you deliver this to the bonding warehouse," Addison said. "You'll have Wybert with you again, just in case, since anybody who doesn't know this Ilount might actually be intimidated by his presence."

Aileen chuckled. That was God's Honest Truth. People who knew Wybert would probably just laugh.

Then they might do something so stupid that the human got involved. Aileen knew about the thing Lazarus called a bracer. She didn't approve, necessarily, but she understood the human's logic well enough. It gave him options midway between surrender and killing.

What the hell did it say about Innruld Space that she even had to consider something like that?

# CHAPTER TWENTY-NINE

## LAZARUS

LAZARUS STUDIED the corridors as they moved through Zhoonarrim Station. Identical to Aceanx, and before that Dormell. And Brasilia. And hundreds of others he had known in two decades space-bound.

There were only so many ways to assemble corridors for tall bipeds like Innruld. The only significant difference that he saw was the fact that no hatch had a lip to step over, like humans stations frequently did. Addison could clear them, but it might be interesting to see how a Qooph handled it. Might require a rolling start and a lot of noise.

The Bonding Warehouse had been typical as well. Stacks of shelves fifteen feet tall, each of them six feet deep, and running a long distance around the station's curve. Giant forklift-style equipment would place the boxes according to some esoteric logic of space, need, and clustering, until the people arrived to pick up their boxes.

They were almost back to *Shiva Zephyr Glaive* now. Lazarus had noted that the corridors also seemed more empty than Aceanx or Dormell. Fewer people moving around, which made a sort of sense if the business cycle was about to collapse along periodic waves.

Living in space was expensive. If you didn't have a job, your savings could get eaten quickly, and Lazarus didn't suppose that the Innruld thought enough of their servant species to maintain a nice safety net.

Too much Hobbs. Not enough Locke.

At least nobody tall and lanky had been following them around. Or waiting at chokepoints with hard eyes. Wybert might look intimidating, but Lazarus wasn't fooled. Aileen was probably more dangerous, just because she knew how to move around tall, heavy things that might tip over on you.

She glanced up at him now, across the empty sled, everyone moving at a Yithadreph's walk.

"So far, so good?" she asked quietly.

"Yeah," Lazarus nodded. "Keep waiting for the other shoe to drop."

"I do understand that feeling," Aileen grinned. "Like a charge of lightning in the air that hasn't grounded out."

And then they were back at the airlock hatch. Lazarus watched Aileen enter a complicated code to open the door and everyone filed inside. He walked sideways as they did, just waiting for someone to come running at them from a side corridor, violence or madness in their eyes.

Nobody did, but that didn't stop him from standing just this side of the hatch as Aileen closed them back up.

Only when the metal sealed did he feel the knot in his shoulders relax. Aileen had the same movement in her shoulders, so maybe it wasn't just him.

They grinned at each other for a moment.

Onto the lift, they ascended back into the relative safety of the ship, but Addison was standing there when they arrived. Or coiled there. Whatever a Churquen did when they stood up on their tail.

The look on his face was not promising.

"Addison?" Aileen asked as the lift stopped.

"Lazarus and I have been summoned by my superiors," he announced in a tight, almost angry voice.

Yes, that was the other shoe Lazarus had been expecting.

# CHAPTER THIRTY

## ADDISON

ADDISON WATCHED the impact of his words on the team that had just delivered the cargo. Aileen's scowl was predictable, but Remahle's snarl took him aback for a moment.

"And they expect us to just accept that?" Remahle growled. "Turn him over to them when they ask, so they can pick his brains for anything he might know?"

Addison turned his attention on the Kr'mari. Noted the tiny hands, designed to hang to limbs and help climb trees, also ended in claws that were half-flexed right now. Pack-sign. Lazarus was one of them, as far as much of his crew was concerned.

But the orders from Eha had been very specific. And they had come from her, so she was on station right now.

Waiting for them.

"Those are my orders," Addison said, trying to keep a lid on things with his crew.

His friends.

"I'm going with you," Aileen announced in a tone that Addison might have used to slice meat.

"You're not cleared for this," Addison attempted to soothe her.

"I don't care, Addison," she snarled up at him. "If Remahle's right and they basically intend to kidnap Lazarus, I'm done flying for them. If you allow it, then I'm done with you, too."

Addison felt his eyeslits snap open in surprise. She was angry. Lazarus hadn't moved from the thing he called parade rest, except that his shoulders and those terrible muscles across his upper chest had flexed. Like he was holding a similar rage inside, but not giving it voice.

Addison considered. It was poor tradecraft, allowing someone into a different cell that they didn't know. That behavior opened up all sorts of risk, but Aileen wasn't bluffing.

"Addison," Kuei's voice suddenly sounded over the intercom. She must have been listening in. "That goes for me and Khyaa'sha as well. You'll need a new crew if your superiors carry through with this."

Addison felt the world drop all the way through his long intestines like a swallowed ice cube that stubbornly refused to melt.

"What you're talking about is mutiny," he said in a very quiet tone. Not an accusation. Maybe pleading instead.

"Yes," Aileen took a step closer and poked him in the chest with one finger. "We're supposed to be better than the Innruld."

"The orders just say to bring him," Addison tried a different tack. "There's nothing that says he can't continue to fly with us."

"If it was that easy, they would have shown up on your deck to talk," Aileen snapped. "Not separated you and Lazarus from anybody that might help stop them from doing something stupid."

Addison didn't have a good response to that. He felt the same way.

But what choice did *he* have? Effect his own mutiny? Tell Eha and her people to take a slithering leap into a river?

But looking into the eyes of these three, he understood that Eha had just put him into an impossible situation. As Lazarus had feared, Addison expected that Eha would demand everything the human knew, and might resort to violence and maybe even torture to get it.

Lazarus would give them the location of the Rio Alliance if pressed, but he might also route them directly to Westphalia without saying anything, and let Eha's people fly into a deathtrap that might cause all of Innruld Space to become fair game.

"You realize it is all a trap, right?" Lazarus finally spoke, in a voice so deep in tone and dark in color that Addison felt his scales flex up like feathers unconsciously. "Aileen's right."

"We won't know until they force it, Lazarus," Addison replied. "The rest is just speculation until then."

"Granted," Lazarus agreed. "But I want you to understand that I'm feeling boxed into a corner much the same way as those seven Innruld did. You're my Director and Aileen's my boss, but I will not walk into a cattle chute without a fight."

Addison didn't understand the terms Lazarus used, but there was no mistaking his intent. Those Innruld had just been punks bullying people. It hadn't ever gotten personal, either way. Just two groups solving a simple problem with violence that the Innruld didn't really understand.

Eha and her people would probably be prepared for trouble. Expecting that they could overwhelm a human on numbers, assuming they didn't just bring in some stun weaponry and beam Lazarus down if he resisted. And Aileen when she fought back. And Addison when he took sides.

Sides.

There were only supposed to be two. Had only ever been two. Humans represented at least two more, depending on how you wanted to count it.

Either way, nothing would likely ever be the same.

"Kuei," Addison raised his voice. "Listening?"

"I am, Addison," she replied immediately.

"Round everyone up and send them back here," Addison decided. "This needs to be a crew-wide thing, if we're going to do it."

Lazarus retained the frown on his face, but Aileen smiled. She'd been with him long enough to know how his mind worked. And could probably read the scales around his chin for cues.

What was the best way to prepare for mutiny?

# CHAPTER THIRTY-ONE

## LAZARUS

LAZARUS STUDIED the room after the bouncer finally let them into what he could only describe as an old-fashioned speak-easy. Locked door with a vision slit in it and some serious deadbolts holding everything to the frame. Vaadwig bruiser protecting inhabitants.

The only thing that threw him off was the smell of tea. His brain kept expecting that whiff of alcohol to permeate everything, but instead herbal hints filled the air. The folks in here were an eclectic mix of species, some he knew and some he had only read about in Aileen's books, like a Zentra, over by the bar.

But Addison had led them to the farthest, back corner. Aileen had found the two of them chairs, hers a stool with a foot ladder and his a folding, metal thing probably meant to make an Innruld uncomfortable, should one actually be allowed in here.

The shopkeeper was a Kdari, another of the leotaur folk like the woman that had won the poetry slam, according to how Aileen had scored it. He wore a tight shirt in green under a black apron sporting various stains, and gray quadrupedal pants that came down to the tops of round boots done in black leather.

The man approached with menus and left them with as much of a smile as Lazarus supposed he and Aileen were likely to get, as the tea-master seemed to know Addison on sight. Fortunately, Khyaa'sha had prepared him, so Lazarus knew what three or four of these mixes would taste like, stuff safe enough to indulge in without risk of poisoning or accidental narcotic overdose.

Aileen seemed more nervous than he did, but Lazarus supposed that she was feeling like she had reached the end of her bluff.

He had known that something like this would be coming from the first moment he came to understand that Addison Wolcott, the intrepid smuggler, was working for an organization. Criminals, rebels, or just businessmen, they would demand to know what value Lazarus might provide, that they could exploit it to gain an upper hand against someone else.

That their enemies happened to be the Innruld that would most likely be getting their due, just meant that Lazarus was more likely to make common cause with them.

*If they asked nicely.*

He silently tapped his left wrist on the edge of the table, just to remind himself that the metal and leather bracer was still there. Aileen noticed the motion and a small smile came as far as her eyes.

Addison seemed distracted by the room, but Lazarus had no baseline against which to compare. He had, however, managed to sit himself in such a way that the front door, the bar, and the doorway to the interior were all in front of him. Wouldn't help him if they came with beams out, but at least they'd be in front of him.

Just because, Lazarus shifted his hands to the underside

of the table, lifting slightly with his wrists to see how much it weighed. And that it was not bolted to the floor.

"Do you think that will be necessary?" Addison asked in a low voice.

"I'm hoping they have the sense God gave a goose, Addison," Lazarus replied. "What I don't know is what form that will take. Do they shoot on sight? Talk until I'm blue in the face? Offer me an actual deal, although they have no idea what I want?"

"What do you want?" Aileen spoke up, watching the Kdari slowly make his way over to take orders.

Lazarus let the interruption frame his thoughts and give him time to think. Tea was ordered and the three of them were alone again.

"Eventually? To get home," Lazarus told her. "Maybe bring an embassy with me to negotiate trade and political alliances against Westphalia. Kind of depends on how this goes today."

He hoped it would go well enough that he could take Addison and Aileen with him. They would probably enjoy Brasilia, he thought. And Addison, or at least Cormac, knew the way back to *Ajax*, so Lazarus couldn't just steal a ship and rely on luck and intuition to get him there. He would need the others, if he wanted to take his own ship home.

Other conversation at their table stopped as the interior door opened and a person Lazarus interpreted as a female Churquen slithered into view, tea mug in one hand and eyes only for them. Addison had started with a quiet gasp when she appeared, so Lazarus assumed that she was the reason they were here.

He looked for goons accompanying the woman, and saw none. No obvious ones, anyway. Nobody was paying that close of attention to them.

He decided not to touch the tea when it arrived,

suddenly too nervous about what someone might put in it. He'd try to find a way to interrupt the others as well.

It would have been nicer if she had brought along soldiers to make an obvious threat, instead of just triggering his paranoia by joining them as if nothing was going on.

Or was it all that innocent and Lazarus had overreacted? But Aileen had joined him out on the precipice, as had Addison, so maybe there was more to it than just him being a stranger.

The woman slithered to the open fourth spot at the table and nodded to him, specifically, before glancing at the others.

"Addison," she turned her attention that way as she coiled herself. "Brought friends?"

"Eha, this is Aileen Enjehn, my loadmaster," Addison replied conversationally, like this was just tea and not a deeper conspiracy. "And Lazarus, who is probably the reason you have come as far as Zhoonarrim to speak with us, rather than sending someone else."

Lazarus rose from his uncomfortable chair and offered her a bow. She might misinterpret a hand out to be shaken, as that wasn't an Innruld thing. What other cultures needed to make it obvious that you were unarmed by offering an open hand?

Eha studied him for several seconds as the tea-master returned with several small pots steaming lightly. After the Kdari retreated, Lazarus reached out with a leg under the table and lightly tapped Aileen with a foot as she reached for her mug.

She looked around confused for a second and then turned her head his way. Lazarus shook his head ever so slightly at her and then smiled at the other two.

Aileen retracted her hands like she had touched a hot stove.

"You seem nervous, Lazarus," Eha offered. "I really did just come to talk."

Maybe so. And maybe she'd been in transit during the time he was on Aceanx, and hadn't caught up fully on all *that* news. He was not feeling charitable, or overly warm.

"Culture shock," Lazarus lied facilely to the woman. "Back home, there are primarily four intelligent species for most of known space. I can see nine in this room alone, none of which I knew six months ago save myself."

"So it's true," she said. "Humans are from a distant part of the galaxy that has never yet encountered Innruld Space?"

"Addison and I believe it is just a matter of time," Lazarus replied, locking his attention on the woman and trying to read her non-verbal cues. "Either one of your ships will stumble into human space, or more likely one of our explorers will come here."

"Is that how you arrived?" Eha's eyes were almost the color of hammered gold. Vertically slit like Addison's. Larger than the Director's and expressive, but she wasn't telling him anything right now.

"I was fleeing for my life from an enemy task force," Lazarus decided to let that much truth out. It would keep them nervous about humans, at least for now.

"Task force?" she asked.

"Twenty-one warships formed up and fighting as a single squadron," Lazarus replied.

He let his mind wander back to the ambush. The sixteen Phalanx-class destroyers of the GunWall itself. Four Archer heavy destroyers being protected. And the CommandWall at the back that had been too prepared for a simple navigational error dropping everyone into the same area at once.

"They were too much for the one warship I commanded," he continued after a beat. "My ship was badly damaged, so my crew evacuated and I fled into trans-space, looking for a place to blow the ship up. It contained secrets Westphalia should never have."

"I see," she said, slightly taken aback, probably at the thought of human war fleets running around in a galaxy that didn't understand what organized war really was.

"After that, I was in an emergency escape pod that was accidentally destroyed on my first encounter with *Shiva Zephyr Glaive*." He smiled lightly to take the sting out of the words. "Wybert continues to apologize, but all my technology was lost, save the suit I was in. Addison rescued me and has offered me a berth on his ship for the time being."

"The time being?" She glanced over at the other Churquen for a moment.

Something passed between the two of them that Lazarus couldn't identify, except that Addison seemed almost smitten by the woman. Was there some level of mating dance also wrapped up in the relationship? How might that alter all these equations?

"It is open-ended," Addison spoke now, his normal voice a little husky, as if to confirm Lazarus's speculation.

"What if we were to make you a better offer?" Eha came right out and played her first card.

Badly, too, since she had no idea what that might constitute. If Addison had told her anything at all of value, she would have most likely approached it differently.

Lazarus smiled and leaned back slightly, using a technique his sainted mother had frequently trapped her foes with, usually over coffee.

You just listened with a vague smile and waited for them to start telling stories and lies. Mother never corrected them at the table. If she liked you, she might ask later, in privacy, for clarification of some point you had made.

But she was most definitely listening.

Many of her bridge buddies had come to fear that smile. Lazarus smiled brightly at Eha and let her talk.

"What would convince you to join us?" she asked quietly, suddenly floundering in rough waters.

Aileen was the only one here that was a good swimmer. She just smiled at the spy as well. Their mothers must have been friends at some point.

"I already work for Director Wolcott," Lazarus offered innocently, nodding to Addison just to see how far he could take her before she twitched.

"There is a larger organization," she offered vaguely, possibly realizing finally how thin the ice under her scales had gotten.

Lazarus scanned the room once, but nobody was paying much attention. Neither he nor Aileen had touched the tea, but both of the Churquen were patiently sipping.

In the back of his mind, Lazarus was waiting for one of them to pass out suddenly. The table wasn't that heavy, at least for a human who was angry and possibly fighting for his life.

"What could I do for a larger organization?" Lazarus let his voice and his face grow more serious.

"You commanded a ship, a warship," Eha said, falling quieter. "And Addison tells me that you were a scientist of some sort as well. We need better technology to fight our overlords."

"Overturn Innruld Space?" he asked, just to see how far down that damning path she might be willing to commit herself. "Bring down the masters? What would you replace them with?"

"Why does anything have to replace them?" her eyes grew slitted and predatory now. Her voice got raspy and harsh. "Or anyone? Can the people not be free?"

Oh, shit. He was dealing with a true believer, not just a

con artist dressed up as a politician, like he had been expecting. Those were the most dangerous ones, because they tended to rely, at least historically, on cults of personality, rather than organized legal structures.

"I would be quite interested in reading your proposed constitution, Eha," Lazarus decided to drop a live explosive into the center of her coils. At least metaphorically.

"Our what?" she asked, head cocking to the side in confusion that seemed to cover all intelligent species.

"A constitution is a legal document that forms the basis of organized government," Lazarus said. "What powers each body has. What things they cannot do. How each serves as a check on the other."

"Oh, the Charter of Dreams," her face suddenly lit up. "Addison should have showed it to you."

"That's a statement of principles, Eha," Lazarus fired right back. "Not a governing document. If the Innruld vanished today, what would you do to govern yourselves tomorrow?"

He wanted to ask more. This woman had suddenly revealed a side that Lazarus hadn't been expecting. He had come here planning to deal with deceptions and spies, not young turk revolutionaries. That sounded too much like the Rio Alliance on a good day.

*Thunk.*

Somebody had just bashed something extremely heavy into the outside of the door to the tea shop. Everyone leapt to their feet, or whatever. Lazarus accidentally knocked the table over in such a way that nobody was wearing scalding hot water in the aftermath, as he set the table down in its side beyond the two women.

A second heavy blow and Lazarus saw seams start appearing around the edges of the door, where the frame itself was starting to give way. The Vaadwig bouncer was standing around lost. Probably never actually been raided by cops with the brains to bring a big enough hammer.

An *almost* big enough hammer.

Eha was as shocked as Addison and the tea-master. Aileen grabbed one of Eha's unresisting, skinny arms and twisted it around behind the Churquen woman's back. Not necessarily the worst thing to do, but unnecessary.

Lazarus turned to the two Churquen. Both were starting to realize that a trap had sprung. It only remained to see whose, but Lazarus didn't want to be here that long.

"How do we escape this room?" he asked Eha in a sharp voice.

"What?" she stammered.

"The authorities are about to kick that door in," Lazarus pointed. "We need to not be here in three seconds."

"This way," Addison spoke up, flowing out of his coil and heading towards the door Eha had emerged from.

Rather than argue, the Churquen woman followed.

Lazarus took a step and then turned to Aileen.

"If we have to run, there is no way you can keep up," he said.

She nodded grimly.

"Leave me behind," she offered.

"No," Lazarus said. "May I pick you up and carry you instead?"

"Can you do that?"

"As long as you don't tickle me, yes," he smiled.

She smiled back and stepped close.

"Promise," she said quietly as he lifted her in both hands. "For now."

"Come on, you two!" Addison yelled.

Eha had already vanished through the rear door. The front was coming apart now as a third blow stove something in. Others were waking up to the trouble and headed this way, but Lazarus grabbed Aileen like a child and used his size and long legs to outrun most of them and hipcheck somebody to the side.

Addison was ahead. Eha was just headed into a door. Lazarus would have liked to have closed and barred this door, but too many folks were following on stubbier legs. Hopefully, he'd be able to outdistance them enough to slam something in their faces yet.

# CHAPTER THIRTY-TWO

### ADDISON

ADDISON SLITHERED as fast as he could snap his coils back and forth, aware that the human's incredibly long legs gave him a tremendous advantage in that realm, too. Churquen were stealth hunters, not chasers.

Eha was right behind him, steering him with flicks to his tail.

"Right here," she said also. "Through this door."

Addison turned and was in an office of some sort, largely abandoned, or just used for transients and not personalized.

Lazarus carried Aileen through the door a moment later.

"Dead end?" the human turned an angry face on Eha.

Addison would have normally stepped in to protect her, but he was feeling some level of betrayal and rage himself.

"No," she snapped. "Do you take me for a fool? Close the door and lock it."

Addison didn't answer what he hoped was only a rhetorical question. He just stayed out of the way as Lazarus slammed the door shut with a heel and then set the lock.

"Help me," Eha turned to him and began shoving a cabinet to one side.

Addison put his coils into the corner and pushed horizontally against the wall. The cabinet moved and revealed a gap in the deck plates with a ladder on one side and a coiling pole down the center. Everyone except Ereshkiki Nisab would be able to escape this way, if they found it.

"Down," Eha ordered.

Lazarus started to move the desk, but only to slide it back to where it was originally as Addison watched.

"You lead," Addison told Eha. "We'll be right behind you."

He looked up at the tall, angry human and tried to gauge the lethality that was sitting on the surface of that smooth, pink skin.

"Thoughts?" he asked.

Lazarus looked down the hole for a moment and came to a decision.

"You two go next. I'll come last," he said. "I think I can pull the cabinet back into place long enough to buy us some extra time."

Addison wanted to say something that even his own mind determined was monumentally stupid before it came out. Churquen were all lower-body strength, with no shoulders to speak of. Yithadreph like Aileen could not lift any significant weight above their head because their arms were so short.

Only a human could do something like that.

Addison nodded instead and clung to the coiling pole, rotating down it into another office on a deck below. What kind of bribes had been necessary to create such a false access? But then, the organization was old. This trapdoor might have been built decades ago, and been in use for people like Eha who needed to come and go.

How much of the organization itself was at risk right

now? If those were Innruld soldiers above them, had they been stalking Eha or Lazarus?

Still, he moved with all the speed he could. At this point, Addison was facing execution if the authorities even suspected him of what he was really doing. Hopefully, they were just trying to capture a dangerous human for questioning or imprisonment by trapping him in a tea shop.

Aileen came next, moving slowly down the ladder set to one side as Addison joined Eha at the door. In his mind, he knew he would need to stop her from just abandoning them all down here in whatever labyrinth she had uncovered. Addison didn't know this level of the station, itself being mostly places for Systems Mechanics to go.

On the one hand, perhaps it could get them safely back to the ship without them encountering guards. On the other, where would he find a map without Eha?

Lazarus started down the ladder, but only far enough to get below the upper deck. Eha reached to trigger the hatch, but Addison caught her hand and held it in both of his as she rounded on him angrily.

"Shh," he said simply, nodding upwards. "Not yet."

Overhead, Lazarus had grabbed that cabinet and was working it across the floor until he had to withdraw his hands from the gap. Then he lowered himself one rung and got under it.

Addison knew he would keep to his dying day the image of the human lifting that incredibly heavy cabinet on his neck and shoulders enough to slide it back into place. He knew how substantial the thing was, and yet the human did it and wasn't even apparently breathing heavy.

*And hopefully, this one still considers me a friend.*

Then Lazarus simply grabbed the coiling pole and wrapped himself around it, sliding to the deck with a fast thump that caused Eha to jump even more than Addison did. Humans were infinitely adaptable creatures, weren't they?

Aileen's grin did nothing to aid Addison's peace of mind.

"Now we go," Addison turned to Eha and said shakily.

Eha scowled at him briefly, but she was just as shaken. He could see that in the way her scales were ruffed up from the skin on her neck. She triggered the hatch and slithered out far enough to peek both ways down the corridor.

"It's clear," she whispered back to him, obviously trying not to stare at the dangerous human as Lazarus picked Aileen up again.

"Go," Addison ordered her.

Lazarus and Aileen would defer to him as Director. Eha would need to get them away, but he could see the seeds of panic in the way she moved. This woman was an analyst, not a field agent. She ran agents in the field, but returned safely home to her invisible life behind a desk.

*Nobody has ever shot at her.*

Eha turned left and started to move, her scales hissing and swishing against the deck even louder than his. Addison had to check behind him to make sure Lazarus was still there.

*And the human moves as silent as any predator, even carrying a Yithadreph in his arms. Scary.*

The corridor they were traversing was dim with spare light. Greasy on the walls with old stains, but the deck was generally clean. The air smelled stale. Addison tapped Eha on the tail as they approached an intersection.

"We need to get to my ship," he said simply as she looked at him.

"What?" her voice started to rise.

"The cargo has been delivered," Addison spoke sternly, trying to use his voice as a lifeline to her fragile psyche, although Aileen might be a better one to do that.

Addison knew he had personal issues that might be

clouding his judgment.

"He's right," Lazarus spoke up. "We need to get off this station."

"If the authorities are really after one of you, do you think they'll just let you go?" Eha snapped, some color coming back into her voice.

"No," Lazarus was calm, deadly certainty as he replied. "But I'm willing to blast my way out of here if I have to. And I cannot imagine that there aren't things we can do that don't damage anything permanently."

"Such as?" she demanded.

"Get us to the ship so we have options," Addison tried to deflect her rage back onto him, someone she had known for years, as opposed to the frightening apparition that had brought her to Zhoonarrim. "We're in the mechanical tunnels under the dock level, correct?"

"We are," she said finally. "This way."

Addison let her move, flowing into her wake. He expected Lazarus to set Aileen down, but realized that the human had the endurance to carry her as well, now up on his shoulders with her legs on either side of his head.

Addison had an image of a human child being carried thus, and knew that humans could do yet another exotic thing so few other species could even envision. And the corridors down here were scaled to Innruld size, so Aileen had the space to ride safely.

*What have I gotten myself into?*

But it was far too late to take that question seriously. Greed and curiosity had gotten themselves wrapped around his tail. Now he needed to see if they could help him escape with the prize that the human represented.

Eha led them down another corridor and looked all directions before pausing. From the coiled stance, she was trying to count bulkheads to the right one.

"We're under dock three," Aileen spoke up now, drawing Addison and Eha's eyes to her.

She pointed up at a sign painted on the roof of the intersection, and then forward.

"Six is that way," she continued with a smile.

At least one of them wasn't lost. Or verging on panic.

Eha started forward with the others in her wake. Quickly, they crossed under part of four and then turned left to circle under five.

Were all of the docks accessible secretly like this? In all the years he had been doing this, Addison had never given any thought to it. They just landed the ship on a tray that was withdrawn into a lockspace. The authorities pressurized the bay and then Aileen loaded everything onto the cargo sled for delivery to the bonding warehouse.

What sorts of smuggling could he be doing, if he didn't have to walk all of his cargo through a customs inspection? What the hell had they been thinking, not to have told him about all this, long ago?

But Addison understood. Secrets leaked. If someone quit a ship in anger, it would be the work of moments to tell the authorities something like this existed. Only in an emergency could they be used.

And today counted.

"Here," Eha finally stopped, breathing heavy from the exertion and stress. Addison was not much better. Lazarus boosted Aileen up and turned her in a front flip to land on her feet, like they had practiced the move.

Did Lazarus have children? The topic had never come up, but the human was also reticent about his personal past, for all that he had shared about Rio Alliance and Westphalia.

Looking around, Addison found a ramp for workers needing to access the underside of a landing slider. He moved quickly up it and determined that there was a hatch at the top, and the light showed that the chamber beyond was pressurized.

He returned to his comrades, focusing his eyes on Eha for the most part.

"Hopefully, we can sneak aboard the ship," he said. "If they are here for Lazarus, it might be safe for you to remain on station, but if they knew to follow us to the tea shop, then you may be the one they were after."

"Agreed," Eha said, finally finding something upon which to base her emotions: logic.

She turned to the human and stared up at him for several seconds.

"You believe that you can free the ship, in spite of being in a contained dock?" she asked.

"And get away with it afterwards, yes," he said simply. "There are emergency overrides that can be accessed on the big doors themselves, exactly for such a situation. We're just going to use them in ways the designers never envisioned."

She turned back to him now and Addison saw fear mingling with the logic.

"Your cover will be permanently blown," she noted. "Many of your contacts will come under increased scrutiny."

"And you yourself may be first on that list, if they know to question a Churquen director," Addison replied. "At the same time, we may be on the verge of ending Innruld domination of the league of species. I am willing to go pirate under those circumstances. Will you join us?"

It was a simple enough request, on the face of it. Her eyes saw the deeper layers underneath. The *running away with me* parts that hopefully the bipeds missed.

They had danced around the topic for years, unwilling to give it voice. Addison knew he was smitten with the woman. He hoped that she felt something similar.

This was the moment where she would have to decide for

herself. Join them, or break his heart.

Logic fled from those golden eyes for a second as he watched. Something else replaced it, but Addison was too fearful to give it a name until she gave it voice.

Eha turned to Aileen, then Lazarus, pausing longer to study the human. Finally, she turned back to him.

"Pirates?" she asked, sarcasm finally evident in her tones. "Why not explorers, Addison Wolcott?"

He shrugged to try to hide his elation.

"Because I expect people to be shooting at us more frequently, Eha Dunham," Addison smiled.

She nodded, and the first hints of a smile appeared in those eyes.

"I believe that the league will need to be better represented than a mere Director can achieve, in that case," she said, laughter appearing in her voice. "Of course I will come with you."

Addison felt his heart start beating again. He hugged her briefly, both arms and coil, before turning to Lazarus.

"Okay, I've just done something crazy," he smiled at the human. "How the hell do we pull it off?"

Lazarus grinned, the warm look without those frightening teeth appearing.

"We get aboard the ship as quietly and quickly as we can," he said. "Then I get into my suit and commit breaking and entering."

Addison nodded and slid himself back up the ramp, checking that it could be unlocked from this side, that there was air over there, and that the scanners didn't currently register anyone standing in the bay itself.

Knowing the Innruld, there would be guards on the outside of the hatch, to keep anyone from approaching via the normal corridors. He wondered if they were as ignorant of the tunnels as he had been.

Probably, if nobody had been down here to meet them.

Taking a deep breath, Addison pressed the lock button and the system beeped to itself, and then to the room, announcing its intent.

The portal slid sideways into the deck and Addison peeked his head above the floor.

Wybert had been standing guard with that stupid powerspear of his. The noise had drawn his attention this direction, but he was still guarding the airlock ramp.

Addison got high enough that Wybert could see him, and then put a finger to his lips for silence. Wybert watched confused for a moment, then nodded.

Addison emerged onto the bay deck and started across the space, gesturing Wybert to board the ship immediately. At least the Ilount goofball took orders well, rattling noisily up the ramp.

Behind him, Eha emerged, followed by Lazarus. Aileen came last, triggering the hatch to seal itself back up in preparation for death pressure.

At least if they succeeded. Addison knew that an alarm had gone off somewhere when the hatch slid open. What he didn't know what who would see it, and who they might tell.

How quickly would someone open the hatch to the hallway and walk in here to arrest him?

As soon as Addison made it to the airlock, he keyed the ship-wide intercom.

"This is Addison," he said sternly. "Prepare the ship for immediate, emergency departure. Oh, and we might be about to become pirates."

He cut the circuit before too many of the cheers came back to him from wherever. Addison knew his crew. Smuggling was profitable, but a passive way to undercut the overlords.

Piracy was a whole different matter.

# CHAPTER THIRTY-THREE

LAZARUS

THE HATCH CLOSED, Lazarus raced across the deck to the ramp, getting to the top just as Aileen cleared the far end. He went through at a dead run, catching the lip at the far side and using that to pivot himself around without slowing.

He also nearly kicked Addison in the head as he did, but the man managed to duck the acrobatics.

Aileen followed Lazarus into the storage area, jumping up and grabbing components while he stripped his T-shirt and kicked his shoes into a corner.

Time was going to be critical. How much did they have?

Naked, he found a box to sit on as Aileen approached with the abdomen base unit with all the plumbing attachments. She slid it over his feet and then turned for the other parts while he stood and pulled it up and into place. Docking wasn't painful, if you took the time, which he didn't have, so Lazarus just grunted as the two plumbing pieces locked themselves into place and gripped for zero gravity and deep space.

Aileen had been paying attention when he took it off.

Boots were ready for him to stand into as soon as the pain of docking went away. Gauntlets next.

She didn't have the strength to lift the chest piece, so he did that while she held his helmet. Six latches down each side, and the various systems came alive.

He had done diagnostics monthly, like you were supposed to, but not put it on since he boarded *Shiva Zephyr Glaive* a lifetime ago.

Back out in the main cargo bay, Addison was arguing with Wybert.

"He'll need someone protecting him," Wybert groused.

"He'd be opening the outer hatch and probably voiding atmosphere," Addison growled back. "Anyone in the bay at that moment risks being blown into deep space. I won't stop to pick them up."

"But it's not fair," the voice got sharp and pained.

"Besides," Addison added. "We may need to blast our way out, so you might have to engage someone with the guns when they start chasing us."

Lazarus liked the way Wybert's eyes lit up. He handed his spear to Eha without realizing it and rocketed off on all ten feet for the ramp that would take him to the turret underneath their deck.

Lazarus locked his helmet into place but left the faceplate open as Addison turned to him.

"That was fast," Addison observed.

"Designed for being put on quickly in an emergency," Lazarus replied. "You really expecting combat?"

"Not at all, but it keeps Wybert out of your way and the guns will remain locked from the bridge," Addison said. "Now what?"

"Now you take yourself to the bridge," Lazarus said. "I go out there and open the bay to space with the manual overrides. You should probably expect the fines to be astronomical."

"The Rio Alliance can pay them for me when we return," Addison laughed and grinned.

Lazarus shook his head and turned to Aileen. He knelt down and got a hug and a kiss on the cheek that surprised him, tickling his skin with her whiskers.

"Be right back," he said heavily as he stood and raced for the hatch.

Out in the bay, the ship closed up quickly as he watched. Lazarus crossed to the control board and studied it for a second before he found the set of controls he wanted.

Why anyone would want to manually vent a bay like this made absolutely no sense, unless a ship sitting here suffered some sort of leak that poisoned the air, but Lazarus found the menu item he needed to start the process.

The main hatch into the station beeped suddenly, as someone on the outside woke up to trouble and wanted in. Lazarus overrode those controls from here and locked it in place, but he had no idea how long it would take the Stationmaster to override him in turn.

And no interest in finding out.

Lazarus triggered the manual alarms that told everybody within earshot that *Shiva Zephyr Glaive* had just suffered a reactor leak that was going to kill everyone who breathed it if they didn't seal themselves up onto bottled air immediately.

On *Ajax*, that was a siren. Here it was more like a large duck choking on a piece of oversized feed that had gotten stuck in their throat. Not even a cat hacking up a hairball was as likely to get inside your head.

Lazarus slammed his faceplate shut manually to cut the sound and told the bay doors to open, venting all the toxic air into space rather than drawing it into the station's supplies and risking contamination there.

He loved engineers. Give them a scenario and then get the hell out of their way as they solved it. The outer hatch didn't creep open like normal. All six slabs pistoned themselves backwards into the bulkheads as fast as their engines would pull with a sound like a meteor hitting the ground. The resulting tornado of air would have sucked Lazarus out into the main bay hard enough that he would have slammed into something rigid and probably broken himself.

Instead, he held tight to the bar that the engineers had designed exactly for someone standing here in a suit to hold onto when the air went away and wanted to take you with it.

God bless paranoid engineers with a sufficient budget to do the job *right*.

*Shiva Zephyr Glaive* came alive as the air vacated the room, marker lights on various surfaces and thrusters starting to lift the ship.

Lazarus realized that shutting the bay down had also cut the artificial gravity in here, so he couldn't run back over. Instead, he launched himself at the ship on strong legs.

"Lazarus?" Kuei's voice came over a line. "What is your status?"

"About to grab onto the side of the ship," he said. "Give me a few seconds before you move."

"Acknowledged," she replied.

Lazarus had misjudged his flight in his excitement. Station gravity even lower than the low setting on the ship, compared to the rest of his life. He was too high and would go right over the top of the ship if she didn't move right now. And if Kuei did she would likely just bounce him off the ceiling as well as the far wall.

Crap.

At least the police were stuck outside right now, until

they could come back with suits and a much better warrant to arrest him, but he might be in trouble.

Every second counted, and he was too high to grab on to anything.

Worse, Kuei must have thought he was on track, because she started her thrusters and the ship began to lift.

Oh, this was going to hurt.

Except she missed. Somehow.

Lazarus watched only the starboard side of the ship come up as he went by, but not the port. Kuei riding it up on her tiptoes, maybe?

Aileen suddenly appeared out of the airlock in her own suit and set her boots to the top of the ship with magnets as Lazarus flew over her head. Even the Yithadreph was too short to grab his leg as he flew, but she apparently wasn't about to try mixing vectors and mass in here anyway.

Instead, she raised what his mind saw as a crossbow and shot him with it.

*Hey, wait a minute!*

But it didn't penetrate his armored lifesuit when it thumped.

Lazarus felt a tug and looked down.

She'd shot him with a clump of glue on the end of a line.

*Huh. Cargo harpoon. Okay, that was sneaky. And brilliant.*

Lazarus felt like a prize swordfish as she stopped his movement and anchored him to the ship. *Shiva Zephyr Glaive* moved then, lifting the rest of the way as he suddenly changed direction as the rope found a new hinge point and started downward.

*Crap, more pain. Going to slam into the hull at speed without the ability to get my legs out first.*

Except he saw the airlock opening. And Aileen had timed her shot and her length of rope just right.

Loadmaster wasn't just a title. It was apparently a calling. Lazarus went into the maw of the airlock like a guppy being swallowed by a whale.

But then, hadn't God cast him in the role of Job?

# CHAPTER THIRTY-FOUR

## ADDISON

"HE'S SECURED," Addison said, watching Aileen demonstrate to the whole galaxy why she was the best loadmaster he'd ever met.

How many others could use a cargo harpoon, momentum, and a moving ship to put a spacer flying the wrong way into an airlock, on the move, on the first try?

"Thrusters coming up," Kuei said aloud, letting the intercom put the information wherever it was needed. "Everybody grab on to something secure."

Addison had his coil pod to sit on, so he just wrapped tighter around it as the ship began to wiggle like a bigger fish on a line than Lazarus had been. Eha was wrapped around a chair normally used by a biped, but she was fine as long as they didn't have to go into combat maneuvers.

He might yet have to actually unlock the guns that Wybert was so assiduously preparing to fire.

*Shiva Zephyr Glaive* came alive, sliding like a Kdari on ice as Kuei fed power to various controls.

You were supposed to move slowly in a prescribed minuet that opened the bay doors and cleared all space for you to navigate into the main courtyard outside, before turning to align with the tunnel headed into the open space where you could engage your engines.

All very precise and organized.

If you weren't turning pirate.

Kuei had probably been dreaming of this day for years, to watch her ears flicker back and forth with excitement. She certainly was pushing the edges of the flight envelope.

Thankfully, there were no other ships in the station's maw as they emerged. That would have been a recipe for disaster.

"Ahead one quarter," Kuei announced.

Addison kept his snout shut and let the tip of his tail semaphore his nervousness. Normally, you transited this corridor at less than one-tenth. But the way was clear and every second of surprise was that much closer to getting away.

Kuei turned to him with a smile Addison could only classify as malicious.

"Chances someone will unlock the station guns before we can get a safe distance away?" she asked.

Addison shrugged in return.

The authorities, someone, had initiated a raid on the tea shop that was an underground front, so they were up to something, but he had not stopped moving long enough to determine if it was just a monumental misunderstanding.

Getting executed was the outcome for guessing wrong right now.

"Permission to get stupid?" Kuei asked with a crazy smile on her face.

Addison thought about it, and decided that he was better off not knowing ahead of time what she had planned. His heart might just explode.

"Do it," he said, gripping his coil pod as tightly as he could.

"All hands, grab on for your lives," she announced with a grand, theatrical voice.

The bow of the ship was in the tunnel now, having maneuvered through the interior courtyard. Addison could see stars and darkness out there, where he knew that Innruld security ships would be scrambling to intercept them at any moment.

Wybert would be proving his mettle by fighting for his life. All of their lives.

And then everything went white.

Addison looked around in utter shock. Not white. Gray. Streaked with blue.

The bridge had not changed, but the light in here had gone from overwhelmed by being inside a station, to the leaden tones of trans-space.

"How is that even possible?" Addison shrieked in complete shock, uncaring what his voice sounded like right now.

Kuei turned back and smiled.

"I have always wanted to do that," she laughed. "The gravity deflection of a station is nothing compared to even a small moon, let alone a planet, so you just have to be lined up clean when you accelerate to trans-space speeds."

"From inside a station?" Addison gasped angrily.

"You wanted a fast, piratical getaway, Addison," she grinned. "Top that."

"Did we just lose Lazarus or Aileen with that stunt?"

He was angry now. Everything would probably come to nothing without the human. And he had known Aileen longer than anybody on this ship.

Except Eha.

"Negative, Addison," Aileen's voice came out of the air. "I knew it was coming. We're both fine."

"Could someone explain to me what just happened?" Eha asked.

Her voice almost sounded normal. Addison took a moment to get his at least as close as hers.

"We just…Kuei just jumped the ship into trans-space from inside the entry corridor of the station," he offered, like it was something they did every day. "It was certainly a novel way to escape police vessels attempting to engage us."

"But I never got to fire at anyone!" Wybert whined like a tired child who has just been told it was bedtime.

Addison laughed, feeling his hysteria fuel it, but he couldn't help himself.

"Next time, Wybert," he half-promised, pretty sure that there would come a time when the Ilount had to shoot something in anger, rather than panic.

"Where are we going?" Eha asked.

"Away," Kuei said. "Not a lot of options in this direction, but it will take them a while to calculate our destination and I don't plan to land anywhere longer than necessary to plot the next course."

"And where's that?" Eha pressed.

"That is up to Lazarus," Addison said, feeling calm finally descend on him like a burial shroud.

# CHAPTER THIRTY-FIVE

## LAZARUS

AFTER AILEEN HAD JOINED him in the airlock, laughing quietly to herself at his ongoing shock, Lazarus stripped back down to nothing and waited for the inner airlock hatch to open. Aileen joined him.

It wasn't like they hadn't seen each other nude before.

"You're insane," Lazarus glanced over as her chuckles threatened to get out of hand. "And you get to clean that goop off my suit."

"Easy enough," she grinned up at him. "Thadrakho has the right solvent. Seriously? You thought you were on your own back there?"

"The thought had crossed my mind," he replied.

"Never," she turned serious. "You're crew. Remember that. We take care of our own."

*Crew. Yeah. Cargo assistant on an alien freighter some twelve hundred light-years away from home, surrounded by species I never knew existed.*

*So this is what home felt like?*

The hatch opened and the two of them stowed suits and got dressed, the beer logo on his shirt mocking him.

He was going to need to get more of them printed after all, beyond the practical joke Aileen had played on that one tailor. Maybe he should start an import business for the humans that came this direction, and whatever other species could handle beer with a four percent ABV. Buy a tanker and haul beer between the stars?

As long as his sainted mother never found out. Better to play piano in a bordello than make beer runs, as far as she was concerned.

Aileen was at his side as they entered the bridge.

All eyes turned this direction, including Cormac, in some bizarre way Lazarus couldn't explain. The NavCrawler had cameras on all sides, but Lazarus felt like those two were looking this way.

"We're away safely," Addison said as Lazarus and Aileen came to something approximating parade rest. "Now what?"

"How crazy do you want to get, Addison?" Lazarus asked.

He noted the way the Director's eyes glanced quickly over at Eha before coming back.

"What are my options?" the Churquen asked as a deflection.

"Sell the ship and try to vanish into the background population," Lazarus offered, just to see the way those eyes got huge for a second as his slits opened like curtains.

They squeezed shut a moment later.

"Not funny, human," Addison growled, but there was laughter under it. And coming from Kuei and Cormac both.

And Aileen. Eha sat frozen, or rapt. Something. Prey look, rather than striking predator.

What did she see when she looked at a human?

"Listing them all," Lazarus chuckled. "Gotta be complete. Second, we can lay in supplies and make the long run to one of the worlds of the Rio Alliance. That will take a while because I have to do a lot of cartography in reverse to find them. Third, you can go pirate. Declare full-on war on the Innruld and see where that takes you."

"We have shields barely better than navigational deflectors, Lazarus," Addison replied. "Wybert's gun was fine against your escape pod, but won't do much against a capital warship. *Shiva Zephyr Glaive* would last about as long as a bushtit against a hawk if we tried it."

"I didn't say anything about *Shiva*, Addison," Lazarus corrected him.

The others missed the significance, but Lazarus had studied the Churquen closely for several months now. Like his life depended on it, which it had.

He saw the realization dance at the back of those hazel eyes before his face squinted hard.

"You're insane, Lazarus," Addison managed to choke out, like he was talking around a rabbit he had just eaten.

"That's always a possibility, Addison," he replied. "But I'm also angry. And tired of walking on eggshells around Innruld who think they are God's Chosen People. If I have to break the Innruld to make the galaxy a better place, so be it. But I can't do that today, so we'll need help."

"What kind of help?" Eha Dunham finally spoke up.

As Lazarus watched, she untangled herself from the chair he had used and slithered closer, forming something of a square with him, Addison, and Aileen.

"He means human help, Eha," Addison spoke before anyone else could. "We'll need to transit to human space and recruit a crew."

"What do you mean, crew?" Eha asked. "What about this crew?"

"It won't be nearly sufficient." Addison looked up at him and Lazarus nodded silently. "Even Wybert's heart isn't big enough to handle what might have to come next."

"He'll try," Lazarus said. "Of that I have no doubt. But you are correct. I'll need roughly one hundred humans in various fields of training. Eventually."

"What are you talking about?" Eha demanded.

"Lazarus, what are the coordinates?" Kuei broke into the conversation. "I only plotted a short jump away from Zhoonarrim, so we need to pivot and jump away again as soon as possible."

"Back into the nebula," Lazarus told her. "Back where we first met."

"It's there?" Addison finally allowed hope into his eyes.

"That's where I hid her before I went and found you," Lazarus nodded.

"Can she fly?" Aileen probed. "You said the vessel was so badly damaged that you had to abandon."

"A small lie," Lazarus nodded grimly at her. "I had no idea who I would be dealing with here. The craft is an experimental bioship. It has been repairing itself slowly since I parked her. Hopefully, she's close enough to done that she can start the journey home."

"Damn it, Addison Wolcott," Eha thundered. "What is going on?"

"*Ajax*," Lazarus fixed her with a predator's stare. "We're going to go get my warship."

"And then?" she asked, suddenly meek as a kitten again.

"And then we're going to hurt people, Eha Dunham," Addison spoke up.

Lazarus nodded.

"We're going to ignite a revolution."

# CHAPTER THIRTY-SIX

AILEEN

JUST BECAUSE THEY were likely to abandon this ship for a long stretch was no reason to slack, so Aileen had Lazarus down in the main cargo bay, doing an inventory. They needed to know everything the ship had happened to be hauling when they went rogue.

Insurance would cover costs for shippers and receivers, because most of this stuff was never arriving at its destination.

Well, never say never, but odds were low. Most of it had just been relegated to junk, using technologies and patents that had no bearing on Rio Alliance engineering.

"Next box?" she asked her burly assistant.

"This one says foodstuffs," Lazarus replied, reading the side of the box.

"Open it and check," she ordered.

She was the loadmaster. He was still just a cargo hand for now.

Lazarus grabbed the wrench and began torqueing bolts open.

"So what happens when we arrive?" she asked absently. "*Ajax*, not Rio."

"Hopefully, the repairs are getting close to done," he grunted as he levered things and pulled the lid off. "This ship is too big to fit into my flight deck, so probably Addison parks it in the same orbit as *Ajax* is holding. Everyone transfers over, and while I start the pre-flight, you and Remahle bring over personal goods and such. Thadrakho starts building ramps where necessary. And then everyone gets a crash course in becoming Rio sailors."

"Just like that?" she asked, disturbed at some quiet level she couldn't quite articulate.

"When we blasted out of Zhoonarrim, that kind of shut down most options, Aileen," he said. "Addison didn't want to break up his crew and send you all off to hide, so you stay together. The word will get around and *Shiva Zephyr Glaive* becomes a rogue vessel to be impounded wherever it tries to land."

"So we're rebels now?"

"You've always been, from what I understand," Lazarus said as he pulled things out and tried to identify the cardboard boxes. "Now it's out in the open. That's all."

"I'm not sure I want to be a revolutionary," she finally found the thing that had been eating at her for the last few hours.

"Few of us ever do," he nodded.

Aileen watched him start to put the boxes away. Candy for someone, special ordered from several planets away. She stole a box for herself before it could go into stores.

"And *Ajax* is a warship, not a cargo hauler, so you won't need a loadmaster."

His sudden laughter threw her off. Lazarus had his head back, howling, leaning on the prybar.

"What's so funny?" she demanded.

It took him several moments to get himself under control.

"Aileen, I had a shakedown crew of nearly one hundred people," he finally explained around the chuckles. "The ship itself was hauling nearly the tonnage of *Shiva Zephyr Glaive* in food, supplies, repair equipment, and personal goods. I didn't have a Loadmaster. I had a Quartermaster, who was in charge of several Loadmasters. I'm hoping you'll take the job, because you're way better at this than any of them ever dreamed of being."

"Really?" she asked, seeing light at the end of a dark tunnel.

"Crew," he said, fixing her with those serious, green eyes. "But more importantly: friends. I have to teach Ereshkiki Nisab and Thadrakho how to run the engines. Addison already knows how to be a First Officer. You were born to be a Quartermaster. I'm not sure how I feel about Wybert being my gunner."

"Dangerous?" she asked.

"I'm pretty sure that with a full crew trained up, *Ajax* could have taken on Zhoonarrim station in single combat," Lazarus gazed down at her with cold eyes. "And annihilated it. Does that tell you?"

"He has a good heart," Aileen spoke up for her crewmate.

"He does," Lazarus agreed. "But he's a little soft in the head at times."

It was her turn to laugh. She'd never heard a more accurate description of Wybert of Capantzina. Lazarus grinned and finished closing the box while he waited for her to get control.

"Addison was right, you know," she finally managed.

"How's that?"

"It's insane, but it will be a grand adventure," she said.

"You have no idea, Aileen Enjehn," Lazarus smiled at her.

# CHAPTER THIRTY-SEVEN

### ADDISON

THEY HAD SETTLED into a routine over the last two weeks, for which Addison was grateful. Eha had been unprepared to suddenly flee for her very life, but had adapted. It helped that Thadrakho could sew her up new shirts and vests from all the fabric they had acquired for Lazarus.

No beer logos, but that was possibly just a matter of time, as his Necherle mechanic turned tailor was making noises about either buying a fabric printer or building himself one from spare parts looted from the cargo bay.

What were the Innruld going to do? Arrest them?

Addison turned to look across the bridge at her. Just look.

Eha was staying in the cabin next to Lazarus on the top deck for now. Addison had not worked up the courage to invite the woman to spend a night in his room, even after all the years he had had such a crush on her.

He wasn't sure he would ever work up the courage. She was his superior officer when they weren't aboard this ship, and he was the Director here when they were. What would happen when they reached *Ajax*?

Several of his spare coil pods had been broken out of storage, one of them installed here on the bridge so she could be comfortable on long watches in trans-space. Cormac could handle the duty, but Addison liked sitting up here and just meditating on space and trans-space when nobody was around. He found it soothing.

Even having Eha here with him this evening didn't disturb that. He glanced over again and found her studying him silently.

They held eye contact for several long seconds.

"So what happens next?" she asked in the most ambiguous way Addison could imagine.

He took the coward's way out.

"We'll be into the heart of the nebula in two days," he offered blandly, hoping she would accept that as the evasion it was and not press. "Then we find *Ajax* and transfer everything over if we can, and head out for Brasilia."

"That's not what I meant, Addison," she snapped, but without any energy behind it. "That much is obvious."

"Then which part were you asking me to speculate about?" he fired back, feeling his scales flex up in just the slightest hint of irritation. All of it was aimed back at himself, but he couldn't help it.

"We go negotiate a treaty and trade agreement with the Rio Alliance?" she tried again. "Risk becoming prisoners or heroes, fools or outlaws, depending on who you ask?"

"I'm already a fool and an outlaw, Eha," Addison said. "What was the purpose of the underground if not to find an opportunity like this and exploit it to try to gain our freedom from the overlords?"

"Are there really that many humans?" she whispered.

Ah. *That* conversation. The same one he and Lazarus had

explored earlier. More humans alone than all other species in known space combined. What would that mass of alien beings do, once they discovered Innruld Space?

"I trust Lazarus on that," Addison said back quietly. "He wanted to originally hide all of us, until I talked him out of it."

"Why would you do something so stupid as that?" her tone grew hot, like a sine wave peaking again. "What will they do to us?"

"Welcome us, I hope," Addison replied. "Every day they get stronger. And their technology might have already surpassed ours, from what tidbits I have been able to gather from Lazarus, so better that we integrate with them today, rather than waiting a century, when Westphalia might have won and those conquerors arrive on our shores intent on subjugating us as well."

"We're risking the entire galaxy," she was quiet again, metronomically walking from fire to ice and back.

She was right. He had only Lazarus as a guide to humanity. Was he one man, or everyman? Was the Rio Alliance a thing, or the cover stories of a spy or con artist?

They would find out soon.

*Shiva Zephyr Glaive* had a rendezvous with destiny in a little over thirty-eight hours.

"If I knew a better way to handle all of this, I would have followed that course instead, Eha," Addison offered. "What would you have me do?"

"I don't know," she said. "I've spent the last several days reviewing all the choices we made. All the steps that led us here, and I can't see where we really had an alternative, from the moment that someone started beating down that door."

She was shivering.

Addison's first response was to uncoil himself from his pod and slither over to comfort her, but he stopped himself before he got very far down that train of thought. Eha had never given him any cues that she had any feelings toward him similar to how he saw her.

All Addison had was his infatuation, since he really didn't even know who the woman was when she wasn't around. He'd seen her more in the last two week than in the last decade combined.

For all he knew, she might have a mate and broods at home. He had never asked personal questions. The less you knew about your fellow spies, the better.

She uncoiled from her pod now and stared at him as if she could see through transparent scales.

"Are you joined?" she asked abruptly, just resting atop her pod rather than holding it.

Addison felt his breath catch. Perhaps her powers also included reading his mind.

"I am not," he stammered back, unsure of himself even more now. "I have been in space for nearly thirty years, never staying long at one station."

"The famous Addison Wolcott?" she said quietly, sliding down from her pod and standing next to it on the deck. "He doesn't have a woman at every station?"

Of course not. There was only one woman who had caught his eye in the last ten years.

"No," Addison held his breath as she flexed a coil and shifted towards him.

A biped would have taken a single, shy step there, to close the distance. She was doing the same.

Addison forced himself to breathe.

"A handsome Churquen like you?" she asked, a little more fire in her voice now as she halved the distance. "Why is that, Addison Wolcott?"

He studied her beauty, those long, amber stripes running down the dark emerald of her scales. The honey in her eyes.

Those long, elegant fingers. The way her tail stretched into a fine tip like a spike, rather than the blunt club of his own.

"You," he whispered so quietly that Cormac might have missed it.

Eha would not. She was suddenly close enough to breathe on.

"Me?" she whispered back, shock registering in her voice. "What about me?"

"You're the only woman I see," Addison decided that he might as well go down fighting at this point, as remain silent. "The only one I have ever noticed."

"You never said anything," she shyly took his hand in hers.

"I know even less about Eha Dunham," he countered. "Are you joined? Broods? Friends? Likes?"

"I have been wedded to the revolution since I was old enough to understand it," she whispered. "You came along later, Mister Impressive Director Wolcott."

"You were my superior officer, Miss Intimidating Spy Dunham."

She giggled, her other hand finding his. They were dancing without moving. Entwining in the eyes, if not the body.

"Shortly, we will be aboard a human vessel," she said, leaning close and kissing him on the cheek. "We will not be officers with rank, but mere travelers. Ambassadors to humankind. We could indulge in ourselves, rather than our duties."

"That is true," he kissed her back, letting go of one hand so it could slide around her back and pull her closer. "I do not wish to wait that long."

# CHAPTER THIRTY-EIGHT

## LAZARUS

LAZARUS WAS STANDING on Addison's bridge as Kuei counted them down. Everyone was here, not just the normal bridge rotation. Even Wybert had given up the thought of his guns to stand and witness history with them.

They would make history today. Again. Second Contact, perhaps. Lazarus looked around at his friends and smiled.

"Ten seconds," Kuei said loudly.

Addison had insisted that Lazarus take command today, navigating them in to perhaps the most fateful rendezvous since an Atomarsk miner accidentally stumbled across a human exploration vessel.

Lazarus looked over and noted that the two Churquen were off to one side, holding hands like giddy teenagers. From the way Addison's scales suddenly flared up from his skin as they made eye contact, Lazarus was willing to bet that the man was doing the Churquen equivalent of a blush.

"Arrival," Kuei said as the smoke and sky of trans-space suddenly gave way to the endless darkness of deep space.

Lazarus hadn't known the orbital period of the ice giant, just the monster's orbital radius out from that distant star.

Roughly five months had passed, so it would not have moved too far. He had been prepared to return perhaps years later when he could finally make the trip.

Kuei had bullseyed the argon green planet anyway. She was that good a pilot. It hung before them like a radiant emerald against the night sky, twice the size of Earth's famous moon from where *Shiva Zephyr Glaive* watched. None of the planet's moons were visible from this range, but Lazarus wasn't surprised.

"Now what?" someone asked. Might have been Wybert.

"Now we sail slowly down to forty-five degrees south," Lazarus said. "She's parked at about fifty thousand miles altitude, above the tiny moons but well inside the more massive ones. Finding a stable orbit was interesting, with so many gravity wells around."

"Will the ship respond to a ping?" Addison asked.

"Not until we get close," Lazarus smiled grimly. "I programmed it to watch near space quietly as it orbited, for the astronomical data, but not to answer any hail from more than one hundred miles away. Safer."

"Moving inward," Kuei began doing her magic on the controls, pressing buttons and moving sliders like a concert pianist. "Everybody might want to go get lunch or something. This is going to take about thirty to forty-five minutes to maneuver around while avoiding debris."

Most of the rest left, back to their regular duties or something, but Lazarus was unable to move even a foot towards the hatch. He would have sat on Addison's coil, but it was a lumpy cone with a blunt top, designed for the Churquen's bottom half to grip.

"Feel good to be home?" the helmsman asked.

"You have no idea, Kuei," he replied. "Many times, I was afraid I would never even return to this system, let alone walk her decks again."

"One person flew it out here," she noted. "Can one fly it back?"

"Yes," Lazarus said. "Once I teach you and everybody how. And redo all the bridge stations for non-humans. And install a translation matrix. Cormac, you'll have the easiest time, and the hardest."

"*Why is that, Lazarus?*" the NavCrawler asked.

"The ship is largely automated, but we don't use Crawlers," he said. "So we don't even have an interface that will work, plus the ship is running on a wholly different technology and language that you will have to learn. Kuei's hands can work the controls easy enough, but Thadrakho and Ereshkiki Nisab will have to build something that will allow you to plug yourself in. And everything will be done at human speeds, rather than what you're used to."

"*I look forward to the challenge, Lazarus,*" the NavCrawler replied adroitly.

They fell into a companionable silence. Kuei didn't talk much, on or off duty, so Lazarus just stood and dreamed.

Eventually, Kuei spoke.

"I think we're there, Lazarus," she said simply, drawing him back into the present. "I'm scanning something at the right elevation and orbit. Shows as a rock, but everything would on my sensors."

"Zoom in and show me," he ordered, suddenly breathless with anticipation.

The main screen changed view as one of the optical telescopes came into play.

There. Yes.

The long, cylindrical hull, with a bulb at the front like goose's head or a spear. The three mighty fins aft, one hundred and twenty degrees apart from each other, housing engines, star drives, and weapon emplacements. They looked almost like flat claws, leaning forward into points where the fronts of the three engine nacelles came to spikes.

*Ajax.*

Lazarus had no words. Apparently his gasp was enough for Kuei.

"Intercept course laid in," she spoke with a smile in her voice. "All hands, we're almost there if you want to see. Channel Five."

Addison and Eha joined them a few minutes later. As did everyone else, rolling, slithering, or walking back onto the bridge and surrounding him. Both Aileen and Khyaa'sha had broad smiles for him.

"That thing's huge!" Addison gasped as the scale came evident. "You said it had a crew of only one hundred."

"I sailed on the shakedown cruise with one hundred," Lazarus corrected him. "*Ajax* would normally carry around five hundred permanent crew, plus a security detachment of troops for ground missions, plus their landers. Or scientists and all their equipment. Another four hundred or so."

"How do we board, then?" Aileen asked. "How do we get all our cargo over there?"

"We've got two pinckes," he smiled at her. "You'll be training to fly one of them."

"Pinckes?"

"Long, narrow, cargo shuttles," Lazarus said. "Stripped down boxes, rather than the nice ship I had. Something like Wybert's truck, scaled up to land from orbit. I took the koch, but those two were both intact when I left. I expect we'll sail the two big ships close together and put them at rest, then run back and forth in the pincke, unloading things from this side into the aft cargo lift like an airlock, loading the shuttle, and then docking it to unload back into gravity."

"How hard are they to fly?" Aileen asked.

"Once I program a few things, you'll mostly just be

supervising," Lazarus said. "They were intended to be brutally simple."

"And the ship is armed?"

Definitely Wybert speaking, even though Lazarus didn't look.

"She's a light starcruiser," Lazarus told the room again. "Built around the Kirov Lance, which is why the body is so long. Most of the beams are actually located out on the pylons."

"How close do you want me to get, Lazarus?" Kuei spoke up into the silence that had overtaken them all.

"About a mile," he replied. "Look for a dark spot right at the front base of the pylon pointed straight down. That's the landing bay."

"That ship is almost a mile long, Lazarus," Addison suddenly found his voice.

"Forty-nine hundred feet, yes," he replied, eyes still glued to the hull, looking for damage that had not been repaired yet.

There wouldn't be any. Not visible, anyway. Five months and change had elapsed since he parked her here. Biosystems would have started on the outer hull immediately and worked their way inwards, taking her back to the external image of the vessel first sliding out of her graving dock, an elegant, sleek, lethality pointed at Westphalia's heart.

Lazarus ignored the curses around him until awed silence fell as they approached.

He knew that *Ajax* was larger than any of the Security Barcs the Innruld forces normally fielded. Only their command pyramids were larger, for size. The Kirov Lance could have dismembered Zhoonarrim Station, so he wasn't that worried about Innruld.

It had taken an entire GunWall to beat him the first time. That and surprise.

He looked forward to returning the favor soon.

But first, he had to have a crew.

Alien. Civilian. Lost at sea. But his friends.

Men and women who had stood with him when they might have just walked away. Didn't matter that they were none of them human. Their love and beauty shown through.

Had not Jesus told the disciples that His Father knew of many other places?

John Fourteen brought him comfort.

> Let not your heart be troubled: ye believe in
> God, believe also in me. In my Father's
> house are many mansions: if it were not so,
> I would have told you. I go to prepare a
> place for you. And if I go and prepare a
> place for you, I will come again, and receive
> you unto myself; that where I am, there ye
> may be also. And whither I go ye know, and
> the way ye know. Thomas saith unto him,
> Lord, we know not whither thou goest; and
> how can we know the way? Jesus saith unto
> him, I am the way, the truth, and the life:
> no man cometh unto the Father, but by me.
> If ye had known me, ye should have known
> my Father also: and from henceforth ye
> know him, and have seen him.

Had he not taken the name of *Lazarus of Bethany* when he was reborn? It had been arrogance itself to adjure unto himself such glory, but he could play some small part in helping these others as they sought the way for themselves. In showing them a better place wherein they might join him in one of those many mansions.

But Jesus had also prepared a place for Lazarus in Innruld Space. Of that he had no doubts, mysterious though The Lord worked. A ship that took him in when he was as Job. Friends that brought him solace and comfort, protecting him from the storms.

He could do no less for them now.

A poke on his arm brought Lazarus back from memories of Sunday Schools of his youth.

Aileen. Yithadreph. Alien.

Friend.

Possessor of a smile at this moment that suggested butter might not melt in her mouth.

"Hmm?"

"So you told me, us, that you took the name Lazarus when you escaped death and magically landed here instead of flying through a star," Aileen said. "If we're going back, does that mean you reclaim your other name?"

Lazarus jolted with surprise. He had walked through the valley of the shadow of death and been reclaimed, so he had put that other name behind him, seemingly forever. And yet, he was about to stride the decks of *Ajax* again.

About to return to the Rio Alliance and claim his place there, along with his experimental warship, his friends, and whatever spy had set him up for death.

"I suppose so, Aileen," he said with wonder in his voice. "I had thought him dead, but God has other plans for me, it seems."

"So who did you used to be?" she asked, fixing him with that look where all the whiskers came forward like lobster claws ready to poke at him.

"Once upon a time, my mother named me Francisco Luiz Oliveira," he said.

Lazarus bowed formally to the woman, unwilling yet to

become Francisco, or even *Pancho,* as many had called him over the years.

Aileen bowed back, just as formally.

"Charmed, sir," she giggled.

Lazarus laughed, feeling belts of tension suddenly loosen. He looked around and found himself at the center of a cluster, everyone touching him and smiling.

"I prefer Lazarus," Addison said.

"So do I," he said simply. "It fits for what is coming."

"And that is?" Aileen asked.

"The beginning."

# READ MORE

Be sure to read all the books in the Lazarus Alliance series!

*Escape*
*Return*
*Rebellion*
*Revolution*
*Liberation*
*Retribution*
*Alliance*

Available at your favorite retailers!

# ABOUT THE AUTHOR

Blaze Ward writes science fiction in the Alexandria Station universe (Jessica Keller, The Science Officer, The Story Road, etc.) as well as several other science fiction universes, such as Star Dragon, the Dominion, and more. He also writes odd bits of high fantasy with swords and orcs. In addition, he is the Editor and Publisher of *Boundary Shock Quarterly Magazine*. You can find out more at his website www.blazeward.com, as well as Facebook, Goodreads, and other places.

Blaze's works are available as ebooks, paper, and audio, and can be found at a variety of online vendors. His newsletter comes out regularly, and you can also follow his blog on his website. He really enjoys interacting with fans, and looks forward to any and all questions—even ones about his books!

**Never miss a release!**
If you'd like to be notified of new releases, sign up for my newsletter.

http://www.blazeward.com/newsletter/

**Buy More!**
Did you know that you can buy directly from my website?

https://www.blazeward.com/shop/

# ABOUT KNOTTED ROAD PRESS

Knotted Road Press fiction specializes in dynamic writing set in mysterious, exotic locations.

Knotted Road Press non–fiction publishes autobiographies, business books, cookbooks, and how–to books with unique voices.

Knotted Road Press creates DRM–free ebooks as well as high–quality print books for readers around the world.

With authors in a variety of genres including literary, poetry, mystery, fantasy, and science fiction, Knotted Road Press has something for everyone.

Knotted Road Press
www.KnottedRoadPress.com

www.ingramcontent.com/pod-product-compliance
Lightning Source LLC
Chambersburg PA
CBHW070518100726
47907CB00004B/884